CI

A Bad Boy Romance

Leah Holt

USA TODAY Bestselling Author
Nora Flite

ISBN-13: 978-1517514280

ISBN-10: 1517514282

Chapter One

Charlie

I could feel his eyes trolling every curve of my breasts down to my hips. Those eyes were black, piercing; darker in person than when I'd watched his trial on television.

A killer before me about to be set free, it made me shiver inside.

Intimidated. That was not a word I was used to feeling, but his presence went beyond just his physical being sitting in the worn chair across from me. He could be felt, a certain intensity filled the air.

Owen Jenkins had entered the prison system at the tender age of eighteen. Now, tcn years later, he was about to cross back into the real world.

And I was supposed to help him.

His hands were shackled to thc table, two feet of chain was all the range he had. My eyes followed the muscular structure of his arms, each curve flowed seamlessly to the next. Ink sheathed the flesh of his forearms, and I wondered to myself if he'd come in with the tattoos, or if they were gained during his time here.

I noticed how even beyond the orange jumpsuit his chest was slightly distended, a common habit for people behind bars. This was a way of saying "I'm in charge." My experiences at the women's correctional facility down south had taught me this was a tactic for survival.

Without it, you'd be eaten alive.

I'd expected the confidence he displayed; his head held high, his shoulders drawn back as if being pulled by imaginary strings, a marionette to the world he lived in.

I felt mesmerized for a moment, unable to look away. He had an alluring magnetism that caused flutters deep inside me.

I wanted to look away, to scan the

concrete walls surrounding us, but I knew as his therapist I had to maintain control of myself. I didn't want him to think he was smelling fear. I needed to dig into my training, use my years of experience to read him and figure out what he was thinking.

That was why warden Lynch had requested me. My notoriety for rehabilitating others had brought me here. But beyond that, I'd felt compelled to take this case; it was a challenge, and that's one thing I love.

I always ask myself before I dive into a new patient:

What happened in your life that made you choose wrong instead of right?

There was always a reason and now, in arms reach of a killer, this question plagued me more than ever.

I was entranced by him. That olive tone skin and strong jaw line, hair as black as his pupils that fell weightlessly across his forehead.

He brought a hand up and brushed it away from his eyes.

He's so handsome, I can't stop staring at him.

Get a grip, he's a patient, Charlie.

I watched his eyes flutter from side to side, but they never looked away from me. He seemed to be trying to figure me out. I was sure he wanted to know what I would ask him.

All of my clients try to imagine what questions will come their way. Picture yourself before a test, not sure what's on it and if you know the right answer. This was the same; except here, there was no right answer.

It didn't matter what I wanted to hear, all that mattered was what was said.

I rested the cold metal of my pen against my lips, trying to push my nerves deep down so I could understand how to approach him.

"Mr. Jenkins, I'm Charlie Laroche..." The words had hardly left my lips when he interrupted.

"I know who you are," he said.

The deep, ominous tone of his voice hit my body, sending chills over my spine.

Shake it off. Control, get control of yourself.

Immediately, I knew I had to be assertive with him. "Then you know why you're here. That saves me some trouble." I was *not* going to let him think he could intimidate me. I leaned back in my chair, trying to appear relaxed and unnerved.

He may be the first male prisoner I've ever worked with, but this wasn't my first rodeo.

Owen sat with closed fists, his breathing slightly heavy. Our eyes were locked on each other, and yet I felt as though he was looking through me, his mind wandering, avoiding any real connection.

Then he turned his head up and inhaled

deeply, his lip curled slightly up on one side.

My pulse jumped.

Am I the first the woman he's laid eyes on in years? Can he smell my perfume? The thought gave me goosebumps. I shifted uncomfortably, my muscles twinging from the thrills.

The energy emitted from him was enough to fill the silence. The light from above gleamed across his brow and I could see small beads of sweat forming.

He's nervous too. Why? Is it me? Do I make him uneasy? I needed to get back to why we were here. I released a slow, subtle breath to try and ground myself. Finally, I said, “I'm sure you know that I read your file. Pretty soon you'll be walking free, that must make you excited. So, let's make our time here worth while. You're part of the new rehabilitation program here for young adults. How do you feel things have gone for you?”

I wanted to know what he felt and thought. I searched his blank expression for something, anything, to guide our conversation towards. You can't hit the tough questions first, always start off light. Too much too soon can close a patient off completely.

Owen sat so utterly still. I looked for a twitch, a double blink, *anything*.

Years of incarceration will either break you or numb you. A prisoner from my old workplace once told me that. Owen was going to be either damaged or shut off. Maintaining some sort of sanity in this environment took strength.

Had Owen been strong enough?

"Well," I asked again, prodding him. "How do you feel?"

His voice was tight. "It's been a long time coming, I deserve my freedom. How do you *think* I feel?"

He wanted control, to ask and not be

asked. His answer, though short, gave me a little insight. He was ready to leave and expected to be set free.

A caged animal released into the public can be a dangerous thing.

That's why I'm here.

“If I were you,” I said, “I'd be excited and antsy. You must have more to say about it than that. I'm listening, so, talk to me.”

Owen jerked his hands slightly. On reflex, my insides jumped. His head tilted to the right and his words muffled out. “Yes, I'm ready for this. I need this. I *deserve* this. I did my time and completed all their programs and shit, this is the end to a long nightmare.” His fingers opened as he spoke, the lines across his forehead lifting. I could see his shoulders slump, a mere trickle of exhaustion setting in.

Finally, I thought with relief, *Some answers. Talking to this guy is like pulling teeth.*

If my report was going to help with his freedom, I needed to get him to trust me and open up. This was a start. “You say you're ready for this, what makes you feel that way?” I asked.

“I don't know, I just feel ready.” He broke the bond between our eyes, glancing around rapidly.

Oddly, now that I wasn't the target of his gaze, I wanted it back. A piece of me wanted to tell him this. Luckily, I'm not crazy. But why the hell was I thinking like this?

He's a convict, a killer! Was that it? The allure of danger? I'd never meet a man like Owen just anywhere. I tried to picture him doing normal things, like grocery shopping, and had to smother a smile.

Shaking off my distraction, I said, “The prison helped you learn a trade skill, tell me what you picked. What grasped your interest?”

“Automotive.” His stare flashed back to

me, turning my blood warm. His voice was clear and distinct.

Mechanics, a smart decision. There are always places willing to hire a convict for the extra tax break that comes with it. "Good choice. What caught your eye about that one?" I was trying to form an actual conversation with him. That was part of my job, it helped me understand the man.

But... my desire to learn more about him went even deeper. It was starting to make me nervous. How was this guy pulling me in so fast?

"Why are you asking me this? Isn't all that in my file you have sitting there?" he asked, gesturing with his fingers. I watched his massive hands as they moved, wondering if they would feel rough against my skin.

Focus, you need to focus. I brushed the hair from my face and adjusted my folders, trying to settle the electricity inside. "It does, but it only tells me what you chose, not why. I want you to tell me why."

"I just like cars, always have. It was an easy pick for me." A light crinkle set across his forehead.

I knew he wouldn't be prepared for this, for me. They never are. No one expects to be asked 'why' to things that seem so minor.

It was a little trick I'd picked up over time. Most people won't open up to someone they don't know, but if you appear to care, they will.

Something that puts me a level up from others in my profession is that I really *do* care.

"Did you spend time when you were younger working with cars? With your dad, or maybe your older brother?" I'd looked into his history, so I knew about what little family he had. Brice was older than Owen, but beyond that, I didn't know anything about the man.

"I had a lot of older friends who had

cars. I liked watching them work on their shit boxes, trying to make them faster or just plain start up at all," he chuckled.

I sat quietly, not breaking the lock I had on his eyes. I wanted him to continue, to give me more detail. People can only sit in uncomfortable silence for so long before needing to say something.

But, Owen didn't look uneasy at all. I felt like *I* was the awkward one. He was so still, his body language unreadable. Before I was able to utter my next sentence he said, "I passed the class with flying colors, so if you ever need a good mechanic, I'll work on your engine." He smirked a bit and gave me a wink.

A hot blush crept up my neck. *I know what he's trying to do. It won't work, I won't let it. He isn't going to get in my head.* I felt out of my element. I didn't expect him to throw an awful pick up line my way, it took all my might to cool the apples in my cheeks.

I sat up straight and crossed my right leg over. I wanted to maintain my professionalism. Quickly, I moved to the next question I could think of. “Do you have plans for when you're free? Any job placement in line for you? Several of my other patients have friends or family ready to help when they get out.”

I had been so wrapped up in his talking, I jolted in my chair as the buzzer went off. It signaled the end to our session, it seemed to be over so quick.

Owen chuckled under his breath. I was taken back by his laughter.

He knows I'm thrown off by him.

I was angry with myself for getting taken in by the man. The way he looked at me, the deep grit in his tone... how he made my thighs squeeze under the table.

This was not how I ran my appointments.

The door opened and the guard came in

to remove Owen back to his cell. I stood quickly, hitting my knee on the corner of the table. The sound echoed through the room loudly, as did my gasp.

I caught Owen's smile from the corner of my eye as I leaned over to gently rub the injury. My heart, already at its limit, began to throb faster.

Then he was gone, his broad back facing me as he was guided out into the hall. The muscles flexed under his orange uniform, rippling in spite of the baggy material.

I rested against the door frame and watched him stroll away. *He turned me into a nervous klutz,* I thought with frustration. *How did he do that?*

I shook my head and retreated back into my office. The solid gray of the walls surrounding me felt cold. I didn't like this place. It had no windows, no warmth.

I missed my old office, it was a much

better environment for my work; inviting, full of color, a place of refuge for my patients. I'd had windows for light and pictures to observe. They all found the change of scenery relaxing.

It's amazing what a little sun can do for someone's mood.

But here I was, in a new prison that was over a hundred years old. It felt like it hadn't changed since it opened. Every wall showed how impenetrable it was.

Even *I* felt like a trapped animal.

I need a plant in here, or something. One single spot of color would make a huge difference.

As I sat at the partially broken desk supplied to me, I gazed at the table that had just held Owen. I imagined him still there, his large, strong hands fixed in front of me. I was revisiting his presence as if I could still feel him.

Our meeting had been only half an hour,

a brief meet and greet. I had also wanted to know what he thought of the program that had basically been started around him.

It was proposed that with the right support, counseling, and education, a young adult on the wrong path could blossom into a functioning member of society.

Owen was the program's guinea pig.

Gathering up my purse to head home, I hesitated. Owen haunted me, his image too easy to call up in my head. He'd looked strong, forearms that were hard as steel. *Would* they feel that solid? I imagined my hand running over the inked surface.

I need to stop this. What am I doing?

I shook my head, trying to push him out of my thoughts. But after my first encounter with the notorious Owen Jenkins, I wanted more. I *needed* more.

There was something I had to remind myself of, though.

The handsome face that had graced me today encased the mind of a murderer.

Even if he'd been found guilty on a lesser charge of manslaughter, the fact remained: he'd taken the life of another man.

He's lucky that he even has the chance to see the light of day again. Why the hell does he seem so... selfish about it? He acts like the world owes him his freedom.

I didn't like his arrogance, how could he not show gratefulness for a second chance?

He was dangerous, he was cocky...

And even so, I felt consumed by him.

It wasn't professional to be entranced in this way, but butterflies flew around my stomach over the thought of seeing him again.

I had to contain this, get focused and keep it. I exhaled heavily as I closed the office door behind me. Walking down the cold cement hall, echoes of my heels filled the space between my ears and my mind.

The main prison gate opened and my face was hit with a rush of cold, December wind. It broke me out of my daze. I wasn't used to this weather or the snow.

I could hear my feet crunch across the frozen ground as I made my way to the protection of my vehicle. *I miss the sun,* I thought, pulling out of the parking lot, trying to avoid the black ice. Down south, we never had to worry about blizzards.

I concentrated on the road, but that damn encounter floated into my thoughts. It was too strong to dismiss. *Why did he seem so ungrateful? Why do his eyes intrigue me? What was he really thinking?*

My mind was a whirlwind of questions. Where were his feeling and emotions? Most inmates I had seen were always so excited.

He was so closed off. But when he smiled at me... I felt my stomach warming over the memory, the light laugh he'd exhaled before he left. All of him fascinated me in ways I couldn't understand and couldn't brush off.

The headlights I passed on my journey home were a blur in my mind, I didn't even remember most of the ride. It was as if my brain had shut off and autopilot took over.

I pulled into the condo development I was staying at. A broad, green wall of shrubbery lined the entrance. The bright yellow of its siding still shined against the white of the snow, even in the darkness.

Greene had been trying to rebuild their community. The town had started new developments to bring in more people, more revenue.

Lucky for me, this is the first one they'd finished. Otherwise, I'd be stuck renting some crappy apartment in a run down building, or staying at the only motel in town.

Dropping my stuff on my couch, I hurried through my end of the evening routine in a haze. Shower, food, then bedtime. It amazed me that the time had flown by without me noticing.

Under my blankets, I found myself thinking about him again. His eyes, though dark and scary, felt deep.

Unable to rest, I threw off the covers with an aggravated groan. Digging into my files, I dropped onto my couch, the papers spread on my lap. If Owen was glued in my skull, then I might as well learn more about him.

Turning the papers in my fingers, I scanned the crisp words. The harsh reality of Owen's crime rested in front of me.

He'd been involved in a breaking and entering at a jewelry store. There, it was reported he'd pushed the security guard down a fight of stairs, killing him. The town had wanted him to be charged with murder. They'd been furious that he'd managed to get it dropped to involuntary manslaughter.

There was also a suspicion that he was involved in a rash of other burglaries, but there was no real evidence. The trial had set this small town on the map; not so much for what he'd done, but for the program that stemmed from it.

In the file, there was a black and white photo of Owen. I brushed it with my fingers, tracing the hard edge of his jaw. I didn't want to be engulfed by him. I definitely didn't want my stomach to tingle as I recalled the intensity of being so near him.

I rested my head back and shut my eyes, hoping these flashes would fade.

I'm his therapist, I took an oath, I reminded myself silently.

And yet, as I drifted off to sleep, the last thing I saw was his smile.

Chapter Two

Owen

Charlie. What a strange name for such a beautiful face.

I stared at the warped ceiling above me. The gray cement blocks were chipping and flaking apart. I'd spent years watching them erode, each day blending together, wondering if I'd actually get to wake up again with the morning sunrise on my face.

In here, there was no sun. There were no birds singing. What we had was the sound of over grown boys carrying guns, telling us when to get up, when to eat, when to sleep. I *hated* that.

The guards think their guns give them power. I knew they were all a bunch of insecure assholes with authority issues. Using the weapon was a way to feel better about their small cocks.

I don't deserve to be here, I never deserved this. One error and I get fucked.

I was left behind, left here to rot like spoiled food in the trash.

My rage was building, I exhaled heavily.

I'll be out soon. I had to keep this in the forefront of my mind.

Images of Charlie began to intercede the negativity surrounding me. These flashes were welcome, it had been ten years since I was that close to a woman.

And a fucking hot as hell woman, too.

Her voluptuous curves replaced the idea of being forgotten. I could see the emerald green of her eyes taking me in, their jeweled surface reflecting my image back. I watched her breasts rise and fall with her breathing.

I could tell by the way she fidgeted in her chair that she was nervous. I couldn't be sure, but I had a hunch that it had been me that had made her squirm. Honestly, I loved that idea.

If she thinks I made her writhe around this time just by looking at her, I'd kill for a chance to show her what I can really do.

Kill. That word made me flinch, so I hurried to think about Charlie again.

Her soft ivory skin, the gentle curls of her burgundy hair resting over her shoulders. She was hot, a real woman for me to lay my eyes on.

I needed her, *needed* to run my hands over her body. Her full breasts called to me, so obvious beneath the light pink blouse that dressed her chest.

My pants tightened with thoughts of her sweet, southern accent as it parted her lips. Immediately I wondered if they'd feel as sweet draped over my cock.

What I'd give to have that, it would be worth the trouble to claim this woman.

My years of being alone here were

almost done. I was ready to feel the warm skin of a woman's beautiful body against mine. No more pretending or dreaming.

She'd asked me about what I planned to do once I was out of this shit-hole. I didn't have an answer for that. I didn't even know what family or friends I'd have left. No one had tried to contact me or come and see me.

I could hear the heavy breathing from the inmate next door getting off. Probably using a dirty magazine smuggled in by another criminal.

Prison was not a place for me.

There are two things you could do here to pass time; work out or jerk off. I guess Hector chose the less sweaty activity.

I looked over at the small collection of books I had sitting on the shelf next to my mirror. Thumbing through them, I realized I had read all of them at least three times each.

A shimmer of my reflection caught my

eye. I stared at myself in the mirror and barely recognized the face glaring back.

I could see the results from my time here. An expressionless appearance, hardened by the brutal world of the prison system.

I fell back defeated on my bed, it creaked loudly as the weight of my body hit it, bowing in the middle where support lacked. I tried to close my eyes and sleep, but Charlie was there.

What questions will she have for me next week? I wondered.

I couldn't stop thinking about all the dirty things I wanted to do to her. I imagined running my hand up her thigh, sliding it between her legs to feel the heat that radiated.

I could still smell her perfume in my nostrils. There was a time where perfume was nauseating to my senses, a choking sensation would fill my lungs. But her fragrance stayed with me. The mix of lilac and vanilla was a refreshing scent.

In spite of my hunger for her, Charlie had an air around her that got under my skin. She seemed to hold herself on a higher level. I didn't like that. It made me feel beneath her.

It was a tough thing for me to grin and bare. I grew up feeling as if I needed approval from those around me, those who were supposed to love me.

My childhood was a sham.

I spent more time trying to seek some form of acceptance from my older brother Brice than anyone else. My mother left when I was two and my father, a raging alcoholic, didn't care what we did or when so long as he was left alone to enjoy his vodka.

If Brice or myself got into any trouble and got caught, dad's good ole leather friend told us just how he felt about it. My father had no mercy.

I always felt my dad had been easier on Brice. I questioned if it was because he was the first born, maybe it had been because I was a mistake?

I just always had it in my mind that I was never wanted or good enough for his liking.

All of that doesn't matter anymore.

I was really hoping that my next session with her wouldn't lead to questions about my family. They're in the past and I'm moving forward. She could ask me anything else, anything at all.

Family life was better left where it belonged.

Forgotten.

The low groan of my neighbor broke my concentration.

He must have finished.

The mattress below me was thin. I could feel every spring as I shifted, trying to get comfortable. I spent most nights dreaming, it was an escape from the hell I'd been living in.

The end was so close, it was in my grasp.

This town had made an experiment of me. On the local news I've heard my story, heard the thoughts the residents had about setting me free.

One gentleman had said, “He won't change, they never do. You can't change a soul that doesn't exist.”

A local woman called me a monster, a pit of emptiness. She said when I'm set free she would make sure to lock her doors.

These people know nothing about me. They only know what the media portrays me as.

And so does Charlie.

I'm an experiment to her, too. A chance for her to get another notch on her belt.

She's just like every other doctor I've seen, only here for the pay check. What would or could be done with someone like me?

Nothing... I hate what I've become.

The lights flickered gently, I heard the soft soles of the guard coming by my cell. A head check for the night. Counting us like live stock in a pen. I couldn't wait to be free, free to live again on the outside.

I was ready to rid myself of being number 995462 and reclaim my identity. I'd realized after the first year that I was really on my own here. No one cared about what I was going through.

That night at the jewelry store played relentlessly in my dreams. A night that should have never happened, a man that shouldn't have ended up dead.

I did what I had to.

My old life was not easy by any means. Things were rough, I lived on the edge, and I took freedom for granted.

I didn't think about any consequences, it never really occurred to me that this is where I'd end up. The day those barred doors sealed shut behind me was an awakening. It became real, not just a threat like I'd heard many times before.

It became my reality.

The walls around me seemed to get smaller every day. I had plastered them with posters, trying to make it feel a little more homey. It didn't help, I'm being suffocated.

The constant yelling of other prisoners was torture. Every man in here was trying to be the leader of the pack. I had learned early on that if I wanted to survive I had to display my dominance.

No one really messed with me anymore, the fear of being assaulted has faded. Every skill I'd absorbed on the street had paid off in here. Muscle ruled the roost, something I had in spades.

I didn't know if Charlie would understand that, to be able to grasp my need for survival. She was probably raised in a happy suburban home, full of loving memories and laughter.

That thought made me bitter. I wanted what everyone else wanted, I deserved that happiness too.

Why couldn't I have been born in a different family, in a different place? I asked myself this question a lot. I spent years running the streets, having to do things to survive.

Once, getting a can of soup as a meal for the day was a lucky moment in my life. That was the one and only thing I never hated about being here, three meals a day.

The lights suddenly shut off, the glow from the corridor was all that lit my tiny space. I watched the guard as he passed by, his shadow elongated against the back wall.

The dull lighting drew my eyes to the stained floor. The cement was a mix of rust and bodily fluids. It made me cringe to think of the things that had happened in this place before me.

Tomorrow is one day closer to my freedom. Focus on the countdown.

I glanced at my calendar, it was too dark to make out any numbers or days but I could feel the closeness. The glimmer from the hall enhanced the previous graffiti made by former inmates. I stared at the tally marks and names engraved on my walls.

I had no idea if any of those men made it out of here alive. I was able to muster half a smile knowing the next person in this room would not see a single sign of my existence here.

I had promised myself I wouldn't let this place break me. Keeping some trace of my former self had been the most difficult thing.

I wanted Charlie to know that, I wanted her to know that despite all the treatment and all the torture I've felt here, I was *not* broken. I wouldn't let this road block in my life finish me.

I wanted her to write that in her report. The parole board needed to know I'd changed, I wanted them to see enough of a difference to let me out.

Let them see me and only me; not the reason for my stay here, not the fact that I had been a killer. I was a changed man, a new man.

Charlie's face came back to focus in my mind. Those lips, I couldn't shake them out of my thoughts. I didn't really want to, I wanted to taste them.

I imagined the delicate flavor of her tongue. The feel of her creamy skin against my face. I wanted all of that right now, this very moment.

I enjoyed thinking about her. It made my cock, I could feel it growing. All I wanted was for her to touch it and stroke it.

The fantasy made this night one of my easiest. I found it relieving to be distracted from the steel bars.

I kept trying to get comfortable, but I continued to toss and turn, trying to find the right spot to fall asleep. Nothing was helping.

My feet hung off the edge, the blanket was barely thicker than paper, and this intense burning I felt consumed my insides. The nights here seemed endless. I didn't know what time it was, clocks were no where to be found; another way for them to display their control.

Power was all they wanted over us.

We lived here on the prison's time, for all I knew it could be seven at night. I was only ever aware of the actual time when I was in therapy, or if we were being served a meal.

I'm already locked in here, what would knowing the time really change?

Nothing, it wouldn't change a fucking thing. I didn't even think half the inmates here could even tell time.

I've watched a lot of guys come and go over the years, all here for various reasons doing time. I never let any of them in close, not enough to truly know me. I always sat separate and refused to speak about why I was here and what happened.

They all liked to talk and tell their side of things, as if it would give them some sort of satisfaction to think others might believe them.

I don't need some drug dealer or rapist to accept me. No one understands what I've gone through, and I don't need them to.

I'm human, we're all susceptible to mistakes. You can't learn if you don't fuck up.

My only weakness was following those who I thought were there to protect me. That would follow me for the rest of my life.

I won't fall into that dark place again. I refuse to.

My head felt as if it wanted to explode. I hated thinking about my past. The pain that turns my stomach is too much to bear sometimes.

I couldn't wait to leave, to feel fresh air on my face. The small things in life have become the ones I fantasize about. All that I took for granted would have a place in the new life I created.

This nightmare will be over soon.

At least I knew that, knew that my legacy was not going to be in this prison. I'd prove I deserved the freedom this fucking program was offering me. The prison wanted to look good, to act forgiving and charitable.

Fine.

I'd take what they had to offer.

I was owed that pardon, anyway.

My hand rested heavily across my forehead as I released a low grunt of frustration. I tried to push all the regret down, away from my inner thoughts. I was sick of feeling it, I was tired of how it took over so easily.

I was ready for this to all disappear,

ready to get back what I deserved. I wanted to live again. I was going to breath life again.

When I finally walk out those doors I would never look back.

This would become a distant memory.

Charlie. I'd like to make some memories with her.

I'd make her scream, make her sweat. If I had the chance, I'd guarantee that *she* wouldn't forget me. No, I'd turn her stiff, professional attitude upside down when I made her quiver and cum in my arms.

Fuck.

I ached for that.

With the vision of her plump lips and syrupy accent in my ears, I settled onto my hard cot and slept better than I had in years.

Chapter Three

Charlie

A cool breeze raced against my cheeks as I crossed the parking lot of the Greene Correctional Facility. It was so frigid, New England weather was much colder than I had ever expected when I uprooted myself from Louisiana.

I stood at the main gate and stared at the massive structure before me. Anticipation began to creep in; today was my next meeting with Owen.

My stomach was in knots with the nerves that flowed through me. I was ready to feel his eyes take me in, I couldn't wait for that. I wanted to hear him speak, feel his voice as it created waves inside me.

I had thought about him repeatedly since our first encounter. I hadn't been able to forget the way he looked, or the way he looked at me.

I wanted more.

Stop, stop this charlie. You have to stop. I brushed the feeling away, I had to keep my composure.

I'm here as his therapist, I reminded myself as I exhaled and continued through the doors.

Warden Lynch was standing at the front desk. A short, pudgy man, balding on top. I noticed he carried himself the same way as the prisoners; distended chest, hands resting on his side-arm in its holster. A visual display of his power for all to see.

“Good morning, warden,” I said as I extended my right hand.

“Ms. Laroche.” He nodded, dismissing my gesture. I'd only met him once since I'd arrived here and we'd never had a formal introduction. “How has your time been so far at G.C.F?” He gestured with open arms, as if to show me all the glory of the prison, a king proud of the castle he'd built.

"It's been good so far," I said as I retracted my hand awkwardly.

"Let me walk you to your office."

I smiled in agreement as we walked past a window overlooking a massive community room. The criminals congregated there for about an hour a day. I hadn't had the chance yet to see it in action until now.

The room was a circle, guards posted above in a caged walkway. The men were all talking and playing cards or dice. Others were watching the television hanging against the back wall. I could see the separation between the groups. All I could think of was a high school cafeteria, each table a different clique.

As I slowed down to observe, I began to hear the hooting and hollering of the men. I couldn't make out one particular yell from another. It reminded me of a pack of wolves zeroing in on their prey, each howl bringing the attention of another to their call.

The prey was me.

I'd realized in my first week that the warden hadn't expected a female therapist when he'd requested me. Though my name was Charlotte, I went by Charlie, and that had obviously thrown him off. His eyes had flooded with confusion the first time we'd crossed paths.

“Ignore them,” he said, “I'm not sure if you're aware, but you're the only female staff we have. You might experience this kind of reaction often. Just don't let them get under your skin.” He chuckled under his breath as he continued towards my office.

I bristled when he said that. Did he think I didn't have the level of control needed to ignore some slobbering, cat-calling guys? I knew deep down I was qualified for this, and even if the warden doubted me, my work would prove otherwise.

"I won't let some barking animals phase me, sir." I hoped that might show a little of my humor and strength.

"While you may be here for the rehabilitation process, take note that some of these men are extremely dangerous and will try to take advantage of you. That kind of... interaction between prisoner and staff isn't just forbidden, it's illegal," he said, narrowing his eyes at me. "We don't take their behavior lightly, Ms. Laroche, and I expect you will do the same."

I was off kilter with his statement. Did he think I wasn't taking this serious? *Or that I'd somehow let one of the men touch me?*

Helplessly, the memory of Owen—his alluring smirk and flexing arms—entered my mind. Would a man like that try to have his way with me?

Would I let him?

No. I'd never let that happen. I inhaled sharply, hoping the warden didn't notice.

I cleared my throat. “Of course, I take these things very seriously.”

“Let's hope so,” he mumbled.

Heat inched along my spine. He hoped so? The warden had obviously read my background information for him to request me. He had to be aware of my seven years in the field.

I prided myself on my work. My mom used to refer to me as her 'mother hen.' My affinity for wanting to help had paid off. It brought me here, it gave me the chance to make a difference.

“I understand these men *can* be dangerous,” I said, following at his side. “My purpose is to make sure your prison gives them the ability to learn the control they need. I wouldn't down play the seriousness of that.”

He shot me a sideways look. “You can't

always teach an animal to behave. You'd be wise to understand that, even with all of your 'understanding," Ms. Laroche."

What an ass, I thought as we reached the door to my office.

"Any thing you need, Ms. Laroche, just let me know. I'm always around." He continued down the hall, twirling a small whistle.

What a strange man. I closed the door behind me, checking the time. It hit me that my meeting with Owen would begin in half an hour. I could feel my palms getting clammy from the idea of sitting across from him again.

I walked into the small bathroom behind my desk. It was a room the size of a closet, barely enough space between my knees and the sink. I wanted to fix my hair and ensure I looked presentable. I didn't want to look like a mess for the appointment.

With my fingers entwined in my hair-tie, I froze. *What am I doing? This is ridiculous.*

Owen is bad news, and here I am, getting pretty for him. I dropped my hair, scowling at myself in the mirror. *I'm not letting him get to me today, I can't. I haven't stopped thinking about him since last week and I need to.*

No more.

I had to take a stand against this school girl crush.

My job was to get the answers the prison needed to decide Owen's release or not. That was my reason for being here, and that was where my focus needed to stay.

A knock on the door startled me. I left the bathroom just in time to see the heavy door open. My eyes were immediately drawn to the massive figure that filled the space. Owen smirked at me from across the room.

The calmness I had tried to regain disappeared while a barrage of butterflies filled my insides. A voice from behind Owen told him to head over to his seat. His size hid the guard that led him there.

"Welcome back," I uttered out, my voice stumbling across my tongue as it tried to find its footing.

Owen bowed his head to my greeting as the guard secured him to the table. He seemed less tense, his body moved more fluidly as he sat.

I felt a rush of excitement as I made my way over to him, settling into my chair. I wasn't going to let him fluster me, not this time.

"How's it going?" I asked while I took out my pen and opened my notebook, making the conscious effort to keep control.

"Same as it has been, things don't change much here." Goosebumps rose across my skin with the richness of his voice.

"Cold?" he asked, his smile broadening as his eyes skimmed my flesh.

"A little, it's chilly out today." I rubbed my forearms with my hands. I didn't want him to think he was the cause of my skin prickles.

“I wouldn't know, I haven't been outside in a while,” he said with a chuckle as he lifted his hands to show me the chains and cuffs.

I let out a light laugh, it took me by surprise. *Stay on track, get down to business.* “So last time you were here we talked a little about your plans for after all of this, I was thinking about that--” I was trying to direct our conversation when he cut in.

“You were thinking about me, huh? I'm flattered.” His smile touched his eyes. “I thought about you, too.” He winked as he leaned in closer, his chest resting over the table.

I was tempted to lean in towards him. The comment filled me with a warmth, I could feel my cheeks lifting to smile and my breathing become heavier.

He thought about me... No. No. Stop. I was not going to play these games. Yet the mere idea I could have crossed his mind made me giddy.

Where had my resolve gone?

I was angry with myself for my weakness. I was running this show, not him.

"Alright, let's keep going. Tell me about your past. What was it like for you as a child?" I'd decided to jump into a tough question, throw him off a bit.

He arched an eyebrow. "You're not from around here, I can hear your accent. Where are you from?" He was avoiding what I'd just asked. His forehead wrinkled up, hands shuffling together as he waited for my reply.

I debated giving him an answer. I twirled my pen on its tip against the table, wanting to make sure I did this right. *I can't give too much info on myself, we can't get too familiar, but a little info could really help him open up.*

"Louisiana," I said, "I grew up in a small

town south of Baton Rouge. How about you? Have you lived here your whole life?"

"Ah, Louisiana, did you ever go to Mardi Gras? I always thought that would be a cool thing to see," he asked as he leaned back in his chair.

"Yeah, I've been to Mardi Gras."

"I bet you had no trouble getting." He glanced down at my chest, his eyes fixed on my breasts.

The butterflies that were patrolling my stomach burst into flames, the warmth spreading across my body. I brought my hand up to the back of my neck and felt the dampness of sweat.

He wanted to work me up?

Fine.

Two could play this game.

Against my better instincts, I gave him a sly smile. "Well, let's just say my neck hurt for a few days after. My turn now, did you grow up here in Greene?"

"No, I bounced around a bit as a kid. Ended up here about two years before all this shit went down," he said as he looked around the room.

"Why did you move so much as a child? Was it because of your parents?" I knew he'd had several different residences, but most of the information from when he was under age was sealed. I wasn't allowed access to it.

I was able to get the basics; his father's name, his brother's name, and any arrests either one might've had. One thing that confused me was Owen had no priors before this incident. That was fairly odd considering the background of his other family members.

"I don't know why," he said. "That's just how it was. Some people move a lot, others don't. It's not really uncommon you know." He leaned on the table with both arms, his eyes sliding back to my cleavage.

A piece of me wanted to conceal myself, instead I leaned in and pressed my biceps into my chest, lifting my breasts higher for him to see. Owen's eyes widened, his stare fixed upon the fresh skin emerging from my blouse. A surge of electricity buzzed through me.

It was intoxicating, knowing how much he wanted me.

I want him to run his fingers across my shoulders, down until he feels how hard my nipples are from the wild aura around him. I... Blinking, clarity hit me hard. *What is wrong with me? God, am I that desperate?*

I didn't remember the last time I'd had sex, but I didn't think I was so eager I'd throw caution to the wind and flirt with a damn convict.

I pushed on, struggling to speak calmly. "Tell me about your brother, were you guys close?"

Immediately his body language changed.

Owen sat up straight, a sternness on his face. “I'm not going to talk about him, so don't ask me again.” He looked towards the back wall, taking in the clock.

His demeanor had changed so drastically. Obviously, that was a sore spot for him.

Owen whispered, “I could smell your perfume for a while after last time, it stayed with me. I enjoyed that.” He inhaled a deep breath through his nose then exhaled a sigh of pleasure.

I swallowed the lump in my throat. “Owen, we need to talk about you, what happened between you and your--” I was unable to complete my question.

He lifted his fists and slammed them down on the table with such force that my pen rolled off. It landed by his foot. “Don't,” he growled.

I was frozen for a moment, stuck in

limbo, unable to move an inch. Forcing myself to move, I bent under the table and reached down for my pen.

Owen did the same.

In that moment, his hand brushed mine. Our eyes met and his finger rubbed my wrist with a soft, sensitive touch. Pleasure rode through my body, tingles shot from head to toe. Quickly I pulled my arm back, abandoning the pen.

He sat up and held out the pen to me. “Sorry, that's just not something I'm going to talk about.”

I wanted to grab his hand, I wanted him to touch me more. That single stroke of his finger was addicting.

Ugh! You can't do this! He's a convict, a murderer! Why am I feeling this? Stop, Charlie! You need to get control. This is insane.

Despite the rage I had just witnessed, I

wanted him. I wanted to feel him, feel his hands against my skin. My heart raced uncontrollably inside my chest. Our eyes were locked on each other, neither of us breaking the stare.

He exhaled a deep breath. “Look, there are some things that I can't and won't talk about. My only reason for being here is to get out early, nothing else.”

Nothing else. Of course, he just wanted his freedom. Still, hearing him say that it was his *only* reason... it cut me a little. Yes, he didn't know me—and I shouldn't want him to desire me—but I couldn't deny some disappointment from his bluntness.

You don't want to be his reason for coming here, Charlie.

Focus.

I considered his reaction again. His face had turned to stone, I'd seen the hurt in his eyes.

Owen's brother had cut him deep.

“Okay,” I said, “he's off the table. What about other family, your dad? Your mom?” I wanted to be cautious with what and how I asked. His reaction unnerved me, but I didn't want him to shut down.

“My mom I don't even remember, all I was ever told was she moved out west and wanted nothing to do with us. My father... well, let's just say he's a waste of life.” His eyes moved from me to his arms, hands interlocking while he rubbed his thumbs together.

“Everyone has issues with their past, with their families,” I said. “I understand that, my family is far from perfect. Why do you think I became a therapist?” I wanted to create a common ground for him, have him see that he wasn't alone.

He shrugged his shoulders while looking around the room. “Am I supposed to just pour my past out for you onto this table? Do you expect me to fill your notebook with stories of abuse so you can rationalize my behavior? Put the blame on them? I don't work that way. I gave you an answer. It might not be what you want, but it's all you're fucking getting."

I was unprepared for that, no one had ever been so candid towards me. I didn't know how to respond, but I made myself speak. "That's not what I expect at all. Your past doesn't free you from responsibility. You chose to kill that man. I'm just wondering what led you there, and if you've changed since it happened. I'm not just here to shoot the shit with you." I added the last part in a crisp, no-nonsense tone. I wasn't going to let him think he could get away with speaking to me however he wanted.

I waited for his rebuttal. My eyes tried to burn into his thoughts.

The smile he turned on was faded. "Ask me something else then, what's the hold up?

The clock is ticking, Charlie." The anger seemed to settle and his confidence returned.

I tapped my chin with my pen, I wasn't sure what to ask. Our eyes locked, searching each other for insight.

"You're thinking too hard," he said. "Don't think, just ask."

I decided to just go for it. I knew he would most likely give me the run around, but it was worth a try. "Why did you kill that man?"

"That was just a matter of being in the wrong place at the wrong time. Which, oddly enough, I feel like right now I'm in the *right* place." His teeth flashed as he grinned, then winked.

My heart that was already charged with feelings, beat faster than it ever had before. The smile he had was mesmerizing. I had to look away, I didn't want him to see the subtle cockiness forming. With no place else to look I glanced down at my notes, hoping my haze would fade.

"Ah, you agree with me," he said as he laughed.

How could I respond? He was right, I *wanted* to be here across from him. I wanted to feel his presence in front of me again. I'd thought about this meeting with him since our last.

Every piece of me wanted to climb over the table and grab his broad shoulders, feel the strength of his arms around my waist. I envisioned him pressing his lips against mine as our tongues entwined.

"Times up," he said. At that very moment the buzzer sounded and I heard the resonant sound of the door.

No, not yet. I'm not done here, I thought to myself as the guard entered to remove Owen. I wanted more time, I needed more time.

I watched him stand, his eyes remaining

on mine. He held his smile as the guard unlocked him from the table, ready to bring him back to his single cell existence.

So badly, I longed for that tattooed beast to just break free, to jump across the room and grab me in his arms. His teeth and lips nibbling over my neck, his scent filling my head until I was lost.

I itched for all that and more.

But, in the end, all I had was that final image of his orange back as he vanished.

Chapter Four

Owen

I could feel the cold of the small, round, metal table through my clothes . A space of mere inches separated my knees from the top.

For the first time ever the plate in front of me looked unappealing. I prodded the small portion of peas, gazing at them without a blink. The sounds of men conversing around me were muffled by my thoughts.

Her skin.

The soft smooth feel and tranquil color of cream had stayed with me.

That brief moment of contact made me want her more than I had ever wanted anything. I hadn't been able to clear the image of her from my mind.

The way she looked at me, her eyes filled with curiosity... the desire she had to figure me out, pick my brain.

It was fucking sexy.

I absolutely need to have her. She got my blood pumping. I liked a woman with backbone. She'd refused to back down when my anger took over, that gave me a rush. No running, no hiding. Charlie had guts.

Maybe it was my attitude, but every other doctor in the past had given up on me.

Charlie hadn't. She'd stayed.

When I had sat across from her, all I could think of was how much I wanted to be inside of her. She was flooding every thought I had. I enjoyed this distraction, it's refreshing to think of something different.

I used to spend my nights dreaming about the outside world, but now they were full of visions of her. I saw her face in my mind like a photo in my grasp, a picture I couldn't take my eyes from.

Whatever it takes, she'll be mine.

I'd never in my life felt such a drive to

have one single thing. As a kid, I'd followed everyone else. I never went for what I really wanted.

I had spent an entire lifetime trying to please others with what I thought *they* wanted.

When I got here, things changed.

To have no one but yourself is a lonely and yet fulfilling feeling. This place gave me the ability to find myself, a chance to truly think about what I wanted for once.

And now, what I wanted was Charlie. Her entire body had overrun my brain, to the point where no other thoughts flowed. I pictured my hands running through her hair and softly down her neck.

Her collar bone... It makes my cock so fucking hard.

That part of a woman's body is the sexiest, it's always made me tremble inside. I can't help but want to nibble on it.

I could see it the other day. The shiny,

red silk blouse she wore had slipped to the side, exposing her bare skin. I wanted to make her body shiver, feel her flesh sweat from the arousal I'd cause.

Was all of this just because I hadn't been around a woman for so long?

It had to be. Why else would I lust for a stranger so quickly?

The muffles around me grew louder. I lifted my head to watch my surroundings for a moment. One of the guards to my left yelled at the cluster of guys in the back corner. I couldn't make out exactly what was going on, I just assumed it was a fight.

There was a lot of that around here, one testosterone driven man against the next.

The yelling intensified until one of the guards intervened. It took the guard threatening to spray them with mace before the crowd dispersed.

Once the multitude of voices faded to a

normal volume, the men scattered around the cafeteria; back into their self-imposed separation.

I looked down at my food, prodding it. I wasn't interested in the commotion, I'd never egged on a fight or involved myself in any disputes.

Normally, this whole meal would be gone in a blink. I was eager to go back to my cell to get away from these animals. But my appetite today was invisible, the grumbles I would normally hear in my gut didn't exist lately.

Charlie filled me, she replaced my need to eat—to drink. I had to have her or I'd starve.

Somehow, I'll claim her for myself.

Otherwise, it was likely I'd go insane... if I didn't starve first.

"Hey, Owen, you see that man?" The voice rose from behind my right shoulder. I didn't answer at first. I'd heard him, but I had been so far in my own head I had to climb back out.

“Owen? You alright, man?” The speaker was a tall, slender man with a nose half the size of his own face. He called himself Vince, and embezzlement was his crime of choice.

His hair was kept short and tight against his head and he had a high-class walk. He always held his arms around his waist, like he was carrying a stack of books.

That's a habit you get as an accountant or banker. It didn't matter what the actual job was, so long as it involved wearing a suit and a lot of money.

After spending so much time here I had a general idea of what any new comer had done previously in their life before. It was all in how they carried themselves. They wore their status in their stride and appearance.

“What?” I asked as I tried to pull myself to the present and focus on the figure next me.

"Did you see that? Fucking Ricardo," Vince said, the last part under his breath.

"Nah, I didn't and I don't really care to." It wasn't my problem, if it didn't involve me I didn't give a shit. I wasn't here to make friends, my only worry was escaping.

"That guy is such a fucking asshole. He really thinks he's in charge of everyone here. Trying to push the new guy around, I don't get it." He began to examine the 'steak' that rested on his tray. "I bet this is rat. There's no way this is an actual piece of meat. I get that we're in here for punishment, but come on. I wouldn't even feed this to a stray dog." He poked his food as if he expected it to jump off his plate and runaway.

"Yeah, well, it's better than nothing," I said.

"Really? Because the way you're staring at it makes me doubt you." Vince let out a deep, raspy laugh, closing his eyes and shoving the unknown piece of meat into his mouth.

I sat quietly, still focused on Charlie as Vince rambled on and on about what he used to eat. The filets, the caviar, all the expensive cuisines that most people couldn't ever afford.

My head nodded as if I was listening, but inside, her face loomed. I couldn't wait to see her again, it was unbearable. I felt obsessed with these mental images, I wanted to see her now.

When we'd been together last, I'd thought about running my hand up her thigh and over her curves. The chance had been there, she'd come so close to me when her pen had fallen.

I wanted to know what it felt like to have her lips touch mine. *Would they be as soft as velvet?*

“Hey, you there?” Vince asked, his words cutting into my daydream.

“What?” I snapped.

"I *said* I heard Ricardo has been causing a lot of problems with that guy Chris, supposedly he's planning something, not sure what yet, but I guess he doesn't like him. I was told he thinks Chris needs to learn a lesson, he doesn't like his mouth." He chewed, his jaw open to expose his teeth grinding down.

I found it ironic that someone with so much class and refinery ate like such a pig.

"I don't really care what Ricardo does, so long as he doesn't bother me," I said.

Ricardo was here for double homicide, he'd gotten two life sentences. He'd already been here for more than twenty years. When this is all you have, you feel the need to own it.

He'd once tried to 'show me my place.' It didn't work in his favor. The guy ended up at the infirmary, while I endured a few days in solitary.

I hated that fucking place.

After I came out of confinement,

Ricardo never glanced crookedly in my direction again. The guy in charge had been knocked off his high horse; my status here was set.

From that point on, no one messed with me. People who had previously snuffed my existence gave me praise. Those who were weak attempted to gain my friendship.

For the first time ever, I was not the man in the shadows.

I had been recognized.

“You say that now,” Vince scoffed. “But when something goes down you'll probably care. I get it, just don't cry to me later that you missed out on something good, I know how sensitive you are,” Vince said as he let out a chuckle.

I laughed slightly at this; he was good for that, always busting my balls. “I'm pretty sure you're the one who's sensitive. If I remember right, didn't you cry when we watched Bambi?"

"No! I had something in my eye, I told you." He shook his head while looking down at his plate.

"Oh yeah, that's right, the eye issue. I forgot that," I said with a laugh.

"And even if I did, there are some sad moments in that movie! Maybe I'm just a man in tune with my softer side." He motioned his hand towards his heart.

"I'm sure that's it," I said with over the top sympathy. Vince gave me a dirty look.

The bell sounded to end our dinner and the guards did their ritual line up to escort us all back to our cells. Vince stood behind me as we walked back. I could hear him breathing from his nose, it sounded like a mouse squealing between two pillows.

His cell was to the left of mine, so I knew that noise well. It used to bother me but after so many years, I was used to it.

The bars clanked shut and the guard released my cuffs. I rubbed my wrists to ease the soreness. The assholes always put those things on too tight.

I wondered if I would still feel their presence once I was free. Didn't they have a name for that, phantom sensations or something? Like when you lost a limb, but could still 'feel' it attached to you?

As I sat on my bed, her face appeared in my mind. Charlie seemed to satisfy my need for relief, an escape from my own demons. She was magnetized, drawing me in the more time we spent together.

She's amazingly tough, I thought to myself. It took a lot to handle a guy like me, I knew that for sure. I hadn't been easy on her, but in spite of that, she kept returning to our meetings.

Her ability to handle me in the way she did... well, it turned me on.

My cock started to stiffen. I loved that she was fierce. It made me ache to break her down, to watch her give in. Challenges are the best damn thing.

She's determined, and she doesn't back down. When I'd told her I wouldn't talk about my brother, she still asked. Even after I lost my cool, she still questioned me.

Thinking about the heat that crossed her cheeks when I flirted with her about Mardis Gras caused my dick to rise in my pants. I grabbed the tip gently and squeezed. I was horny, I hadn't had a real woman in years.

I laid back and couldn't help but start to stroke my swelling shaft. I wanted to touch her body, I imagined her tits pressed against my chest, wondered if they were as firm as they looked.

There was a fierce need inside of me to feel her pussy warming from the touch of my fingers. I pulled my cock out to stroke it; it was solid, ready to be gripped firmly as my hand slid up and down.

I imagined I was back at her office, no chains, full range of motion with both arms. I wanted to grab her and pull her in, run my thumb down her cheek and over her chin. I would see her lip glisten after her tongue ran over it, ready for me to kiss her.

Quicker, I pumped my shaft, picturing how I'd grab her blouse and tear it from her breasts, exposing her soft, supple nipples for me to suck. I wanted to run my tongue over each one, feel them harden against my lips. I could see her tilting her head back and moaning, wanting me to keep going.

My erection was in full force, my fist strengthened around my length. I pretended it was her hand wrapped around me, my eyes closing tight as the dream continued.

Charlie gripped forcefully around my hardened member, it was ready to explode. I could see myself sucking her tits, squeezing them between my hands, her body arching with excitement.

I would run my fingers over her stomach and across the top of her panties, teasing her, waiting for her to force my hand inside them. Her hips would sway with anticipation, my fingers reaching for her dripping pussy.

I have to fuck her, I need to feel that pussy wrapped around me.

Heat rippled down into my belly. Panting, I ground into my own palm with desperation. Groaning through my teeth, I fought to stay silent while the pleasure turned my core into a furnace.

Charlie... fuck, Charlie!

I exploded all over my hand. The warm ooze flowed down my palm, tension leaving me in waves. *Shit!* I thought as I realized I hadn't prepared for this self gratification, I had no rag for clean up.

Fuck it. Doesn't really matter, it's just me in here.

My body was loose through every muscle; a good hand job does wonders for the mind. I would have preferred having Charlie in the flesh, but the fantasy would do for now.

I can't leave here without making her mine at least once. I'll get what I want, I need her. That woman was all I dreamed about from the moment I woke till I drifted into sleep.

She's going to be a challenge, but one I'll conquer.

I shifted around until I found a sock stuffed between the bed and the wall. *This will do.* I cleaned my hand and threw the sock down next to the sink.

It was late, the lights had gone out a little while ago, but no hint of exhaustion rested in my body. My mind was in a state of turmoil over how strongly I wanted Charlie, how essential it was for me to have her.

I couldn't leave here without getting my way with her.

I wanted more... so much more.

But once would have to do.

All these years I'd waited for the day I would be free, that was what drove me. Charlie drove me now, she gave me energy and desire and too much heat inside my body.

I had thought my lust for freedom could never be shadowed by anything else.

I was wrong.

Chapter Five

Charlie

The chime went off as I entered the Coffee Bean. I had an hour before I needed to be at work. A good friend of mine, Sara, was meeting me here so we could catch up some.

I had gone to school with her, we'd had a class on group therapy together. After school she'd moved here, to Greene.

Seeing her would be a relief. It's a good feeling, having a friend so far from home.

I glanced around the room, looking for her recognizable red mane. I'd never been here before. The walls were pasted with famous people, bright red chairs were perched at every table. There were multiple outlets against the walls of each nook.

This place has some character for a coffee chain.

"Hey, Charlie! Over here!" Her loud New

Yorker accent filled the room. Sara stood and waved me over. Every head in the coffee house turned, their attention on me and my friend. Around here, the folks were quiet and reserved.

They weren't ready for women like Sara.

Sara had a very different type of personality for this area; she was bold and outspoken. Here, everyone talked behind closed doors. It was an old school town were whispers crept as you walked by.

We both had a tendency to say too much. I think that's what made us such good friends.

“Hey lady, how are things?” she said as she leaned in for a hug.

“Ah, they're good I guess.” My nose wrinkled when I spoke the words. I had so much conflict with the feelings I had for Owen. I knew I couldn't tell her about it. It was unethical for me to have any desire for him at all. Unethical, *and* illegal.

But I couldn't stop thinking about him.

She blinked, holding me by the shoulders. “What's wrong?”

“It's nothing really, just the usual stuff. New job, new town, new boss. A whole lot of changes for a southern girl.”

“Yeah, well, it could be worse,” she said with a hollow laugh. “You could be in the midst of an ugly break up, like myself.” Sara released me, toying with her hair. “Frigging jerk, doesn't call me for two days and *I'm* the bad guy. I don't think so.”

I bit back a small smile. “Isn't this the third or fourth time you guys split?”

“It's the third, but that's not the point!”

Eyeing her pout, I shook my head and chuckled. “You really are something. Well, I'm sure you guys will work it out.” As much as the world around me might have changed, other things stayed the same.

“Yeah, we probably will,” she said. “I

guess I love him. A little.” Her laugh echoed through the building. Again, every set of eyes turned to us. “So tell me about your new job, how do you like it? I can't believe you're working there. That prison is creepy, even from the outside.”

I watched her pour three sugars into her coffee and sip it. “Still have a sweet tooth, huh?” I had to say it, the woman had been sweetening everything for years, even her vegetables. It was no wonder she was so high strung.

“Ha! Yeah. It's good, I swear. I don't just do it to help me get through the morning.” Sara squinted at me, pointing with her coffee cup. “Don't change the subject. How's work?”

“I like it, it's definitely different. I don't really care for the warden, but overall it's going well.” I wanted to yell, *I have a crush on an inmate! I can't get him out of my head!* But I couldn't do that. She would definitely disapprove, and probably smack me.

Maybe I should tell her, I could use a good slap to bring me back to reality.

Even the mere idea of touching—god, fucking—Owen was breaking a major rule for patient and doctor relationships. I really wished I could tell someone what was going on in my head.

“That's it, huh? That's the reason you give me when I can see things for you suck face? I don't buy it. When you're ready to tell me, let me know.” She sipped her espresso and rolled her eyes. Sara knew me too well, she'd realized I wasn't being honest.

I sighed violently. “It's complicated, let's just leave it at that.”

We spent the rest of the time catching up on her social life and laughing about our college days. It felt good to have my mind redirected for the moment. I was relieved to be thinking about something other than him.

Yet, he still weighed on my thoughts. The issue was just paused for the moment.

Glancing up, I saw the room was clearing. The morning coffee rush was over, but that meant… "Shit! What time is it? I have to be at work for eleven." I glanced down at my phone and saw I had fifteen minutes to get to the prison. "I have to go, sorry! We need to do this again!" I stood up swiftly and frantically grabbed my things.

She jumped up, sticking her arms in her coat. "I have to go too, I'll walk out with you."

We exited to the street, getting blasted by the cool air. The snow fell at a steady pace, a thick layer already covered the ground. The road was hardly visible beneath the white blanket that coated it.

"I'm over there." I pointed to the right. Just then, I noticed a small dog briskly walking across the street in my peripheral vision. He looked mangy, most likely a stray.

Poor thing stuck out in the cold. I hated seeing pets without a home. Who would abandon an animal like that?

My ears pricked at the sound of tires squealing. In front of me, a car slid into the intersection. I knew something was wrong when it twisted, losing traction as it glided on the snow.

I watched in slow motion as it barreled towards the defenseless dog.

No!

I threw my purse down and burst into the road. I pushed myself, desperately trying to reach the dog before the inevitable happened. There was no care for my own safety. In that moment, all that mattered was the frail animal.

I'll save it, I have to! Oh god, please!

My eyes grew large and my heart raced as I watched the dog make a feeble attempt to run out of the way. His small feet tried to scramble, but the icy conditions made it impossible.

A high pitched whimper split the air.

I was too late.

The car slid into a snow bank, coming to a halt with a metallic crunch.

My heart sank in my chest. Not once did I slow down, I hurried until I neared the body of the dog. From the corner of my eye, I watched as everyone ran to the aid of the driver. They helped push the vehicle out of the snow, but no one was coming to help the dog.

Somehow, the responsibility had fallen to me.

Kneeling down, I touched the cold, shivering body of the animal. It was a small dog, some sort of mutt. The white fur on its side was stained with blood.

I had almost forgotten Sara was there until she crouched beside me.

"Wow, that was crazy, huh? Is he alright?" she asked as she rummaged around through her purse. Her tone was much more casual than I would've expected.

"Sara, call the animal hospital, let them know I'm on my way with a dog that just got hit." I removed my scarf and proceeded to carefully wrap him inside it.

"Charlie, it's just a stray. Don't you have to be at work?"

I glared up at her, forehead knotted, saying nothing. She could see how concerned and upset I was. Immediately, her demeanor changed.

Plunging her hand into jacket pocket, she pulled her phone out. "Okay, I'm calling."

Turning back to the animal, I curled it in the scarf and pulled him to my chest. I didn't care if he was a stray or not, he was a living creature. I couldn't leave knowing he needed help.

I carried him carefully over to my car. He was breathing heavily in my arms. A soft whimper escaped as he looked up at me.

"Don't worry, I'm going to get you help," I whispered as I approached my vehicle. I rested him delicately on my passenger seat.

I hope he's going to be alright. Poor thing. I softly pet the top of his head, his eyes looking up at me in distress. Tears welled up and fell as I looked down at him, knowing he was in pain.

Hopping into my seat, I turned my key in the ignition and sped as quickly as I could down the icy road. I wanted to floor it, but I didn't want a repeat of the earlier accident.

On the drive to the animal hospital I pulled out my phone and dialed the prison. "Glen, it's Charlie. I need you to cancel my first two appointments today. I'm going to be late."

When I was kid, my grandfather owned a farm. I would go visit every summer and I always loved helping with the different animals. As much as I enjoyed my profession, there was a special place in my heart for animals. They didn't have a voice of their own, they couldn't ask for help if they needed it.

If I thought about it, there was a connection between those creatures and the people I sought to save.

The drive felt like it took forever. Finally, I pulled into the hospital parking lot. Carefully lifting the dog back into my arms, I shoved out of the door. My knees were still wet from the snow and slush on the ground.

I can't believe this happened. I'm going to make sure he gets everything he needs. I really hope the injuries aren't too bad.

"You're going to be okay, shh." I tried to console the whimpering dog. Kicking the front entrance open, I ran up to the front desk.

The staff member there looked up at me. "What can we do for you?"

"He was hit by a car and needs help right now!" I shouted, clutching the ragged, dirty dog. Tears had left streaks down my cheeks.

The hospital worker reached out for him. It was hard for me to pass him off, my grip tightening around his frail, quivering body.

He's so helpless, how do I know they'll give the same attention to this lone dog as they would to a family pet?

"My name is Dave," the staff member said calmly. "We will take good care of your dog. Please let me see him." Reluctantly, I did so. "You said a car hit him?"

My hands dug into my jacket. "It lost control on the icy road."

Dave nodded, making me wait as he carried the dog into a room. I was anxious, so when he returned, I jumped forward. "Will he be okay?"

"He'll be fine. Let me get your information, okay?"

Dave took down my name and number so he could call about how the dog was after they examined and treated him. Inhaling until my chest hurt, I felt drained as my adrenaline faded. Then, I spotted the clock above the front desk. It was already noon.

Shit, I need to go!

As much as I wished I could stay to be there for him, I needed to get to work.

My body fell like dead weight into the driver's seat of my car. I couldn't believe how my day had turned. *I hope they call me soon with an update.* That sad, injured face haunted my mind.

Before leaving the hospital I glanced at myself in the mirror. The traumatic event had left me looking ragged. *I can't go into work looking like this.* Black was smeared halfway down my cheek bones from my eyes, my hair was twisted in different directions and wet from the falling snow.

As I fixed myself quickly, the empathy I felt for the dog swam up again. It was overwhelming. *He's going to be fine, he's getting help.* I took in a deep breath and tried to calm myself on the ride to the correctional facility.

I walked briskly into the prison, my adrenaline starting to pump again. *My brain is going to be fried.*

My feet, still wet from the snow, hit the marble tiles. With a sharp gasp, I twisted, trying to keep my balance. Gripping the wall, I puffed out a breath, smoothing my shirt. I had been distracted trying to adjust myself that I almost didn't notice Warden Lynch.

He was rested against the front desk, talking with the clerk. I could already feel a headache brewing, the last thing I wanted was to see him, or to explain why I was late. He would most likely think it was ridiculous and irresponsible for me to put a stray dog before my obligation to *'his'* prison.

He held his coffee mug up to gesture

hello at me, then continued with his conversation.

I smiled and hoped that would be the extent of his greeting. When I passed him without any questions, I breathed a sigh of relief.

I made my way down the corridor towards my office. I had started to approach the community room and could hear some loud yelling coming from inside. When I reached the glass windows that overlooked the area, a large mass of men were yelling and fighting.

The guards posted inside were standing motionless. I tried to understand what was happening.

There was a small man cornered against the back wall by seven men. A large crowd of other prisoners surrounded them, antagonizing the group on.

The guy in the middle was definitely the leader, he was laughing and jabbing the defenseless prisoner. The others around him followed in suit. Each one took a turn to spit on the smaller guy.

He looked frightened and kept glancing up at the guards as if waiting for them to do something. I felt the same as I looked down on him. *What are they doing? Why aren't they stopping this?*

The man that led the attack had a ragged scar across his throat. He seemed to be encouraging each of his cronies. He would point at one of them and they would take their turn.

Each assaulted him in some way as he covered his body, trying to block the blows. The man in charge ran his hand over his greasy black hair as he laughed uncontrollably.

A short, fat guy with a shiny bald head grabbed the injured prisoner by the back of his neck. He pulled his arm back and released a punch into his stomach. The leader patted the fat man on his back as he stepped away, making room for someone else.

This is awful! He can't defend himself against all of them. It's disgusting that they're all finding this funny. Where is the humor in this?

I couldn't believe what I was witnessing. The guards all watched from above and said nothing. They made no attempt to intervene. I raised my hand to the window, about to pound on it to get their attention. I wanted to yell to the guards to do something, or even just draw the attention away from the weak prisoner and onto myself.

They should be controlling the situation. How can they just stand and watch so carelessly? Do what you're getting paid for, assholes!

Right as I lifted my hand, I saw the group of observers part like the red sea. A figure walked effortlessly through the mass of men.

Those who where following the main instigator backed up completely. The leader didn't notice at first and continued to throw blows at the cowering man.

The room fell silent. I heard the soft muffle of a voice. The unknown figured had turned and I could see his side profile.

Owen. That's Owen.

My heart skipped a beat. He pointed at the scarred man who had been beating on the prisoner. The two of them exchanged words. I couldn't hear what was being said, but the gestures said it all.

Owen pointed towards the hurt prisoner and then at the big man in front of him. His eyebrows were crinkled low over his eyes, he definitely didn't approve of the behavior these guys had displayed.

The aggressor tried to get close to Owen's face, he shoved him and Owen barely moved.

I was in awe of his strength, to be there taking a stand, to not back down to the other man and hold his ground.

In a burst of speed, Owen thrust his open hand into the guy's left shoulder. Then, he began yelling and pointing towards the beaten man who was now curled up on the floor in pain.

He's protecting him. He stopped the attack.

My body got chills. Here I was, standing and watching this supposed bad boy show a tenderness that I had not expected was there. I was mesmerized as he shoved the other guy across the room.

No one else joined the fight. Even the guards just observed, not willing to give any assistance.

Owen was in charge.

As the fight ensued, the leader raised his

fist and took a swing at Owen. He was clearly enraged by the fact someone would stand in the way of him and his victim.

I found myself cheering inside my head for Owen, hoping he would knock this guy out. My face was pressed against the glass, knuckles turning bone-white.

What am I doing? This isn't me. I don't like fighting.

But his body language, his sternness, was giving me butterflies.

I'd seen several fights at my old job, but this was different.

This didn't feel pointless.

Owen grabbed the man by his arm and threw him down. He jumped on top of him and repeatedly punched him, one fist after the other. It wasn't until that moment that the guards finally intervened.

They swarmed the two men like flies to a piece of meat, their guns raised in an effort to gain back their control.

It took three guards to get Owen to the floor. He was cuffed and brought to his feet, glaring down at the now bloody and bruised scarred-man. He mouthed a series of words that I couldn't make out.

I wanted him to look up at me; I pressed my palms against the glass, willing him to look in my direction.

He never did.

The main attacker stumbled to his feet, wiping the blood from his nose. It smeared across his cheek as he spit more onto the floor. His eye already showing signs of swelling under the lights.

A smile crept across my face. I wasn't a fan of violence, but that guy got what he deserved. It made me happy that Owen had put himself in danger, just so he could protect someone in need.

Maybe he isn't such a bad guy. Maybe

there's another side to him.

I was more intrigued by Owen than ever before. I was anxious to talk to him, to ask him why he'd saved that prisoner from the others.

Why did he put himself in that position? He didn't need to.

I replayed the scenario in my head. The way he'd stood as still as stone, refusing to back down. He took control when the guards who were here to maintain order couldn't. I could see his muscles tense while he spoke, enhanced by his dark mood.

I ached to have those arms use their strength on me. The thought gave me chills.

Never in my life have I been so wrapped up in someone, and a damn murderer at that! I pulled myself away from the glass, I had to find the warden. Maybe he'd allow me to have another session with Owen. I didn't want to wait a week.

I needed to see him now.

There was more to his story than what he'd let on. A stone-cold, egotistical man would be unconcerned about what others did around him.

What motive did he have to intervene? *Why?*

His noble action deserved praise, he should be commended for saving someone else.

I don't understand, in the past I would have been disgusted by anyone who thought fighting was the answer. But watching Owen just made me want him more. I can't figure myself out, I have no idea why this made me excited. What is going on with me?

The desire to talk to him was overwhelming. I entered my office and immediately called the warden, Lynch. I waited impatiently for him to pick up his line. I hoped he wasn't still congregating in the foyer.

Abruptly, the line clicked as someone picked up. “Hello?” Lynch asked, sounding bored.

"Warden? It's Charlie. I need to set up an extra session to see Owen Jenkins."

"I'm sorry Ms. Laroche, but Mr. Jenkins is in the hole for the next two weeks due to his little stunt in the common area."

My heart stopped. "Wait, what? Why? He didn't..."

"Ms. Laroche, it's our policy here that any inmate who takes part in a fight spends a designated amount of time in the hole. You will return to your normal schedule and see him on your regular day in two weeks."

Gritting my teeth, I went to argue. Before I could try, the dial tone filled my ear.

I was baffled. Owen didn't start that incident. How could he be sent into solitary confinement for something he'd stopped? It didn't make sense to me. The warden didn't have the whole story!

Some lie had been told to the man,

maybe a guard covering for his own lazy ass. I'd had a birds eye view of the whole situation, and Owen hadn't started any trouble. He'd put himself in the middle of danger to help someone.

All I wanted was to see him. I needed him to know I'd seen what he'd done. I was overcome with wanting to help, but I felt impotent.

I stared blankly at my desk. Absently, I let the phone fall back on the receiver.

How has this day gone so wrong?

The suddenly loud ringing jostled me out of my daze. On reaction I picked up the phone. Holding it to my ear I asked, "Hello?"

A piece of me hoped I would hear *his* voice on the other end. I craved the deepness of his gritty baritone.

"Hello, is this Charlie Laroche?" It was not a voice I recognized.

"Yes, this is Charlie."

"My name is Dr. Phillips, I'm calling about your dog. I don't have a name down here for him, but I wanted to let you know he was doing well. He sustained a broken back leg and some bruising to his ribs. Let me just say you, have one tough dog."

I sat up straighter in my chair. "Oh, thank god. You have no idea how happy that makes me to hear that."

"You should be able to pick him up in three days. We'd like to keep him till then, just for observation. So long as nothing pops up, he can go home."

Chewing my bottom lip, I sat forward. "Well, actually, he's not really my dog. I explained all of this to the staff earlier today. I don't know who he belongs to, I just happened to be there when he got hit. He could be a stray or maybe a pet that got loose?"

"Ah, okay. Well, we'll post some things and contact the animal shelter."

Animal shelter? I know what happens to unclaimed dogs there. They don't last long. I don't want that! Maybe I should take him in? Could I take him? No. I barely have enough time for myself, he'd be alone constantly.

I was relieved to know he was fine, he was lucky it was just a broken leg. I tried to move my thoughts onto the only good thing that had finally shined through today. My heart rose a bit to know his injuries were minor.

The dog had a chance at a new life. I was sure some nice family would adopt him and he wouldn't be fending for himself anymore.

The man on the line said, “I want to thank you for doing this for him. He wouldn't have made it out there alone.”

“It was nothing,” I said warily. “Call me when he's better, okay?”

“Of course. Have a good day, Miss.”

The call ended, and instantly, I rested my head against my hands. *I'm always in limbo*. I had to wait to find out about the dog, and about Owen.

My thoughts returned to him, how he was in the hole and I could nothing about it. Even as his therapist I had no authority and no say in what happened to him.

My fist came down hard on the desk. *How does this help his rehabilitation? It just isn't fair to him. That warden has no idea what this could do to him. Complete isolation for that long could take hold of him mentally!*

The purpose of the program was to help give Owen the tools to be part of society again. The treatment was meant to ensure he had the ability to make proper decisions.

How can I do my job when they don't even evaluate a situation like the fight? They just automatically throw people into solitude without knowing why.

This didn't sit right with me. I had a natural instinct to help those in need.

Owen needed me.

And I need him.

Chapter Six

Owen

I couldn't see a foot in front of me.

The only light I had came from a small crack beneath the door. My food was pushed in through a slot, it came at random times. No contact was allowed with anyone, not even the guards.

It was my own private hell.

As I sat in the shadows I could hear a constant dripping of water around me. Echoes of it rang off the pipes and filled the air. It definitely seemed louder than it should be.

I felt so alone, I couldn't even see my own shadow. There could have been another person sitting directly in front of me and I wouldn't even know it.

Punished, again, for trying to do the right thing. That seemed to be a common event in my life.

I'd been shoved into exile for taking a stand; that was a real punch in the gut.

This is why I stopped trying to help.

It always backfires.

And I always fucking pay.

I could feel the pain bubble up again. I hated thinking about what had brought me here to begin with. Desperately, I shoved it back down into the pit of my soul.

But my past kept clawing back up.

It had been my desire to help that had kept me by his side. That, and my damn need to be appreciated–told I was worth something.

I used to tell myself that there would be a time that *he* would take me seriously. He would finally see I knew what I was talking about. I'd thrown myself into harms way a multitude of times for the only one I ever truly felt connected to. The amount of dedication I had to him was numbing.

I'd held him high above me and ignored

the voice inside my head.

Look where that got me. Who's here for me now? Not a soul.

As I sat alone in the dark, realization sank in that I'd been my worst enemy. I was blind to those around me and their motives.

How could I have been so fucking stupid?

I should have never gone that night.

My instincts had been right, they usually are.

I lifted my arms up and grabbed my head, clutching my temples between each forearm. To know things didn't have to end up this way was hard to swallow.

My arms tried to squeeze this regret from my mind. I pressed against my skull, wishing the thought would burst out.

The shittiest part was knowing that I had been left behind by someone who I thought would *always* stand by me.

The pit in my stomach felt as empty as the room I was confined to.

I told him things didn't feel right.

I'd wanted him to change his mind, but...

My brother refused.

Brice had fucking refused.

He was dead set on going forward with the plan. I should have just gone home, but I couldn't leave him there. I'd always put him first above anything else.

Even above myself.

I'd thought I would always have him there for me, that we stood on the same pedestal together as equals.

What did I get for standing by my brother? This, this fucking life behind bars.

Abandoned by the one I'd set out to help. Nothing could cut deeper.

I knew I'd made some awful decisions in my life, I'd chosen the road that led me here, but I didn't have to. I'd had options!

Why didn't I take them?

When I first got into the prison, I'd made endless calls to him. I wrote letters constantly, but never got one in return. He hadn't even attempted to pick up the phone. There was no effort on his part.

Shock had hit me first. Depression set in when I acknowledged that the one person who said they would always have my back had turned against me.

There's no other pain like betrayal by your own blood.

I brushed the sweaty strands of hair away from my face. *My freedom had been taken, my life has been altered forever*, I thought morbidly.

The walls seemed to engulf me, the quiet was maddening. You have to really enjoy being your only company to survive this kind of hell. Otherwise, you'll be the death of your own soul.

I was going to go crazy in here. At least out there I had things to keep me busy.

Charlie had become my new hobby.

Even though I was blind, the image of her face was bright. I wanted to focus on her, push the other thoughts away. I didn't want to think about my brother anymore.

I pictured myself softly touching her hair, the silkiness sliding through my fingertips. My eyes closed as I rested my head against the cool, damp wall. Trying to soak up her silhouette, I squeezed my eyes tighter.

Stay there, stay right there. Don't fade into the wickedness of this place.

I knew that wouldn't be completely possible. The never ending absence of light brought the worst images to my mind. I wanted to think about her, but I couldn't. No matter how hard I tried to keep her curvy figure in my eyes, his deception replaced it easily.

He was my brother. My kin. The one and only person I'd ever been able to rely on.

Apparently, in this fucked up world, you can't even trust your own blood.

If he would've just listened to me for once in his life! I grunted loudly, slamming my foot against the dirty concrete floor. *He failed me, he left me here... left me to rot while he continues to live on the outside.*

That night, there wasn't even supposed to be anyone there. I gritted my teeth in anger, a screeching noise filling my ears. Brice had told me the security would be gone before we arrived. He'd assured me that no one would be inside.

I trusted him.

Like countless times before, I let him lead me into the belly of the beast.

I never thought he would have been ungrateful for what I did. If I could go back and change things I would. I've had dreams about that, being in that place and asserting myself. Not asking him, just making him leave.

In the surrounding abyss I heard muffles of voices outside the door. A shuffle of feet scurried by as I watched the light dim and reemerge from the crack.

A web brush against the back of my neck. Quickly I swatted it away, I hated spiders. Nothing creeped me out more than the thought of a gross, hairy eight-legged creature crawling over me.

My body shivered with disgust. I shifted uncomfortably to try and move away from it. I wasn't even sure if it was a spider, but I wanted to be as far from that feeling as possible.

When I was eight, my brother and myself had decided to camp in our backyard. We only had our sleeping bags, no tent. It was just the two of us, as it had been my whole my life.

I woke up to a burning feeling running

through my entire body, an immense pain that I had never experienced before.

During the night a large recluse spider had crawled into my sleeping bag. It had bit me several times and my entire left leg swelled. The scream I let out was gut wrenching. Brice picked me up and carried me into our house.

His face was plagued with worry and concern. He had been the only person to ever show me that. To show me true care and love.

Our dad was passed out and despite how much Brice tried to wake him, he was dead to the world. Finally, my brother called the ambulance and got the help I needed.

He had saved me.

I had to spend a week in the hospital from that. I've hated spiders ever since. Beyond that, the way I looked at my older brother was never the same. He became my role model, a hero in my eyes. I would have done anything for him.

I *did* do anything.

I gave my life, my freedom, my world to get approval from him.

And here I am, trapped in this place. Why didn't I do things different?

I had spent hours thinking about that single question. When you're young you never think about how your choices can affect your life. The impact that one single decision can have on your entire existence is mind blowing.

I curled up against the corner on the floor. I couldn't see around me; there was no bed, no seat. The only other item was a filthy toilet.

I had never been in confinement this long. I had spent three days in here my first month because of Ricardo. *And here I am again because of him. I hate that fucking bastard.*

I had no idea how long it had been. Time blended together with the lack of light. I had thought about keeping track, trying to figure out a way to tell how much time had gone by.

My attempts were useless. The food came once a day, all three meals at once. There was no rhyme or reason to when it was delivered. It came when they wanted to bring it.

I tried to listen to footsteps, see if I could tell shift changes or breaks. It was no good.

Growling, I punched the wall in frustration. The roughness of the cement split my knuckles open. Warm blood trickled down my hand, I shook it as the throbbing sensation set in. My hand beat as if it was a heart, the pain surging through my arm.

I'm a fucking idiot. I can't let my anger get the best me. It won't help.

I knew I wasn't really angry about being in the hole. I was angry at Brice. It pissed me off that after everything we had been through, he'd stayed away from me.

I'd thought that I was doing the right thing. For once, I could pay him back for how he'd saved me.

Brice was money hungry and greedy, he ran with the wrong crowd, but in the mess of our lives he had always been my brother. A great brother, even with all his faults. In the grand scheme of things I felt he deserved my homage to him.

I can't do this to myself anymore. Why should I care so much about that? I made my choice for a good reason. I gave him a second chance. I just hope he used it wisely.

I wanted to think about Charlie. I thought if I could just fill myself with her, then he would disappear.

She had beautiful wide green eyes. Their gem like resemblance was alluring. *Could she be thinking about me being down here? Stuck like a lab rat in a maze, no way of escape as I slowly crack?*

That's what this place was for. The hole was meant to break people, bog those of us down who they deemed a threat. I knew the warden didn't want me to be set free. No one wanted me to walk the streets.

Everyone fears me and who they think I am. I understood the feelings behind their fear.

To those on the outside, I was a killer.

I wondered if Brice had seen my trial on television. *Did he regret his choice? Does he wish he could change things?*

Brice was five years older than me. Early on, he'd become a figure of authority when our father showed he could care less about us. Brice shifted, taking on the responsibility and struggling to keep me from feeling like no one cared about me.

He was protective, smart and sly. As I got older I tried to follow in his footsteps.

What a mistake that was.

I should have walked outside the path

he'd taken and made my own route. But I hadn't, and here I was.

The look in his eyes that night showed me he never truly cared. I saw an emptiness in them that I had never let myself see before.

I hated replaying that night in my head. The subtleties of his mannerisms should have shown me his motives. “No Owen, it's fine. Don't be a fucking pussy. Get the fuck out of the car and let's go!” he'd yelled at me when we got there.

It wasn't until I was cornered in the back vault that I realized he had no plan. It was a horrible feeling to have, even now; to know that your brother had led you into the flames.

A split second was all I had to think, to act, to give back to him.

All for nothing.

The throbbing in my hand had lessened, but my fingers had swelled. I tried to open and close them but it hurt too much. I hated when I lost control and my rage took over, I saw red sometimes, and that was terrifying. It had been a challenge to keep myself in check. I knew I had a short fuse. The biggest issue was thinking about my past. With those thoughts, the rage would grow.

The breathing techniques and the counting exercises I had been shown were a crock of shit. The only thing I found that actually worked was pushing all those feelings and thoughts deep down. I'd locked them inside and struggled to forget about them.

The doctors all said I needed to deal with it, then move past it. But I *couldn't* deal with it.

I needed to forget it.

How could I listen to their advice when none of them understood me? No one took the time to truly see what happened.

They called me a murderer.

I wanted to laugh in their faces, and a

few times, I did. I couldn't help myself. To have a guy in a white lab coat try and break down who and what they thought I was? Who wouldn't find it funny!

Yup. Sure, it was my defiant testosterone that got me here. Fucking quacks. I cracked up inside with that shit.

A tickle emerged across my arm. Without thinking, I slapped my hand down and killed the spider. A sharp pain shot through my hand. I dismissed the ache and slowly opened my palm to brush the bits to the floor.

If only it was so easy to wipe away my hurt and betrayal.

My brother was never a hero.

And, even worse...

He never once said thank you for saving him.

Chapter Seven
Charlie

My nerves had been running wild all morning. The bowl of cereal I had poured turned soggy as I just sat and stared at it. I found myself scooping the mush, only to drop it back down into the thick milk that resided below it.

I'd decided to toss my breakfast, I couldn't eat. Even if I tried I wouldn't be able to hold down any food.

It was time for my first meeting with Owen since he'd gotten dragged to the hole. It seemed like ages since my eyes had graced his face. I couldn't wait for him to walk through my door.

I was ready to feel his presence. The days between seemed never ending.

I missed him.

I couldn't believe that crossed my mind.

I shouldn't feel this way. Missing him was crazy.

My stomach felt like it was in my throat. There were so many questions to ask. I wondered if he thought about me while he was in there. Could he feel me thinking about him?

I can't believe I'm this nervous. What the hell, Charlie? Get a grip! I thought as I stared at the door waiting for Owen.

A heavy breath escaped my lungs as I tried to gain some self-control. I began to rub my hands against my skirt to erase the sweat that had formed. I felt foolish over the way my body had been reacting.

This is crazy! Settle down.

I glanced up at the clock, there were twenty minutes left before he would be here. I had been given a longer session with him today, an extra half hour. I was excited to know I had more time with him than usual.

The parole board wanted me to extend

our meeting after his little stunt in the community room. With it being so close to his release they wanted to make sure he didn't take any more risks.

They needed to know he understood that what he did was wrong and it could really mess up his release. The hearing had been delayed a week already because of that fight.

I knew he had helped someone in need, but they wouldn't hear what I had to say. I was just told to save it and put it all in my report. I was getting really fed up with everyone around here not listening to what I had to say.

My report was going to lay it all out for them, I knew what I was doing.

I was really turned off by the fact that everyone was so dismissive of his actions in that room. They wanted to know nothing. All they cared about was that he fought someone, that was it. The reason was unimportant.

It seemed everyone around here was

aiming for his failure. I looked at the facts and tried to find the truth. He intrigued me to the point of obsession. I hadn't been able to get him out of mind since day one.

I needed to see him, hear him, talk to him. I knew that time would be soon and I was ready. I watched the second hand tick by on the clock, I glared at it, wishing it to move faster.

I leaned back in my seat, fiddling my pen between my fingers in anticipation. My whole body felt wired just waiting for him.

The lock on my door rang as it jetted back from its security. It opened, and in my mind it seemed like slow motion.

In the doorway I was faced by the outline of his figure. His mass blocked the hall lighting, it shielded his face in a shadow. I could feel my breathing getting heavier before Owen even stepped into the room.

Here we go. My legs trembled like they were cold. I sat up straight and crossed one ankle over the other, hoping it would ease the shaking.

His face gleamed under the florescent lights of the ceiling as he entered. The aura he emitted over took me. Our eyes locked on each other, Owen's appeared brighter than I remembered. The hair that usually draped across his forehead had been combed back tightly.

Wow, he looks refreshed. Not as worn as I expected.

There were two guards with him today.

Huh, that's strange, normally there's only one. I bet it's because they see him as a threat now. Or maybe they just want him to feel even more powerless in their grasp.

His eyes were fixated on me as the larger guard secured his thick wrists in their place at the table, the other fastening his ankles to the floor.

A smile tried to spread across my face. I

used all my effort to keep my lips retracted. An outpouring of butterflies filled my stomach. *Look away. Just look at something else, don't get pulled into him.* I quickly glanced down and brushed my hair behind my ear.

The two guards turned and walked towards the door, but only one of them exited.

The other remained.

"Thank you, I'm all set here," I said. I didn't understand why he was standing inside, positioned like a soldier at the gate of a castle.

He glanced my way. "I was told by Warden Lynch to keep an eye on the prisoner, I'm supposed to stand in today."

What the hell is the warden doing? Is he trying to screw up his therapy? Having that guy in here won't work. I'm done letting Lynch try to rule every aspect of this place. Out there they were his. In here, they are mine.

"First, the prisoner has a name, it's

Owen, and no. That's not how this works. I have patient doctor confidentiality. You can't be here."

"I have orders to..."

My eyes narrowed as I cut him off. "I don't care what you have, you need to leave. If Warden Lynch has a problem with that then he can come talk to me." I couldn't do my job if I had another set of ears in the room.

I'm done biting my tongue. I'm sick of the warden trying to snake his control into my office. Enough is enough.

I never would have stood for this at my old job. I was done playing nice.

Regardless of Owen's reason for being here, despite the fact he was killer, he was *my patient*. I was committed to that first and foremost.

A deep chuckle filled the room. I glanced over to find Owen laughing while shooing the man out with his hands.

The guard stood, dumb founded; he didn't know what to do. I walked over to the door and opened it. “Go, I don't need you here.”

He was hesitant at first, but he stepped into the hall. I closed the door and for the first time locked the emergency latch. It was there for my safety if there was ever an issue inside the prison.

It was necessary for our meeting today. I had no idea if the warden would try to send any guards back in, or end the session because I'd defied him.

I didn't care, I had a job to do.

My heart beat rapidly inside my chest. I couldn't slow it down. I knew Owen was watching me, his eyes following each stride I took. I loved the rush he gave me. This was exactly what I had wanted.

“Long time no see,” he said, winking. It was his calling card, that single flirtatious wink.

I smiled and looked down towards the floor, my cheeks flushing with warmth. “Yeah, it's been a while, huh?”

I had trouble meeting his eyes, I didn't want to show my excitement. I cleared my throat and adjusted my blouse while I walked back to my seat. I tried to focus, bring myself back into therapy mode.

“Nice.” His head cocked back as he let out a slight laugh.

“What?” I asked.

He gestured towards the door with one finger. “That, kicking his ass out. Good move.”

“Well, I need to be able to work. Did you want him in here? His big ears listening to us?” My eyes rolled exaggeratedly.

“That depends.” His smile broadened as he relaxed back into the chair, his eyes engulfing me.

“Depends on what?” My brows lifted with curiosity.

"Our conversation, do you want him to hear about how much you missed me?" he said as he leaned, his chest meeting the table's edge.

He's teasing me, he has to be teasing me. I tried not to show the surprise on my face. I couldn't believe he'd said that. I knew that *I* had wanted to see him, but how could he know?

He's trying to manipulate me.

I smiled made myself laugh. "Alright, obviously the hole has gone to your head. How have things been since you came back to the light?" I wanted to humor him some, but also try to keep this on track.

"Things don't change around here. It's the same as before. Some walls, barred doors, assholes floating everywhere. The usual." Owen shrugged his shoulders, his lip arched up on one side.

"But it won't be that way for much longer, so long as you don't do anything stupid to jeopardize it again." I wanted to see how he reacted to this. I knew what I had witnessed but I wanted to hear it from him.

"No worries about that. I'm getting out of here. No more fighting, scouts honor." He raised three fingers on his right hand as he laughed under his breath. "I was never really a boy scout, but I'm sure you figured that."

"Yeah, I didn't see that in your file." My lips formed a partial smile. "You want to tell me what happened?"

"Not really, it's done. Time was served in the hole and now it's over." His arms crossed across his chest as he leaned back.

My nose wrinkled in frustration. "I get that, but what happened?" *Come on! Stop avoiding my questions!* I was getting annoyed that he kept talking around what I had asked. "You know, I saw the whole thing." I hoped this would jostle him a bit. He wouldn't be able to gloss over any details.

His eyes grew with wonder. He had no idea I had watched the whole thing unfold before me. Sitting in silence for a moment, Owen's head hung down towards the table. "What, did they show you the surveillance tape or something?"

"No, I was walking by, I saw what you did. I tried to talk to the warden about it."

"And? What do you want me to say?" His tone was low while his mouth remained tight. He held his hands up as if to say, 'You caught me.'

He doesn't want to explain why. I'm basically saying I know he didn't do anything wrong, so why isn't he excited about that? He should be reeling to fill me in on what was said and why he stepped in.

"Why did you put yourself in the middle of that? You had to know where it would land you. That it could impact your hearing." My hand fell down on the table. I wanted an explanation.

Owen's eye brows shifted up, his forehead wrinkled. “Sometimes you just have to take a stand.” He paused briefly. “Like you did earlier with the guard. Which I'm not going to lie, that was hot.” A crooked smile emerged over his hard jaw.

I couldn't stop my lips from turning upwards. *Hot? I took charge, I had to. He's right, sometimes it is necessary. It's not always a bad thing to disobey the rules.*

Sometimes they need to be broken.

I still wanted an answer from him. “You helped that prisoner, you didn't have to, but you chose to. Tell me why.”

“It *doesn't* matter why. I just did.” His hands closed into fists as he spoke through gritted teeth.

He's getting pissed. I don't want him angry, I just want him to keep talking. I ran my hand through my hair, unsure how to guide this conversation in a better direction. “Alright, well, was being in solitary for him worth it? Was risking your freedom worth it?” I asked.

“Why does it matter? I'm not going to do it again. Though, since it gets me longer sessions with you, I might consider it.” He brought the dark centers of his eyes my way. I could see them follow the outline of my face, then move down the exposed part of my neckline to my chest.

An automatic sensation of tingles flowed through my body. I wanted him to keep looking at me, but I knew it was wrong. I adjusted my collar to try and draw his eyes back to mine. *No. I can't be feeling this way. Stop it, it's not right.*

I had noticed his hand was wrapped in a white bandage. It went from his knuckles down to his wrist. His fingers were slightly swollen.

“How did you do that? The fight?” I pointed towards the injury.

"Nah, a wall got in my way." He lifted his hand up and wiggled his fingers. "It still works fine, want me to show you? I can give one hell of a massage."

I wanted to yell yes to him. I wanted him to touch me so badly. The idea of his hands running over my skin made me wet.

Stop! I need to stay professional. But I want him to touch me. I want to have his hands all over me. To just reach over and grab me, pull me in close. I want to be wrapped up in his arms.

No. I can't think like this.

He whispered, "I absolutely will, if you like. It would be my pleasure, you look like you could use one, anyway."

I had been silent for longer than I realized. My mind wandered into the dark side of my desire. I didn't know what to say. A piece of me wanted to just straddle him, not say a word, and to feel his lips pressed against mine.

I should end this, I can't be thinking this way. It's dangerous, I can lose my job, my license. I have to end it now, this is too tempting. I've never felt this way towards a patient. It's too much to continue.

"Owen, I'm sorry, we need to stop this here." I stood briskly and took a step towards the door. "We should just pick up next week. Your parole hearing is next Friday, we can meet one more time before then. I'll set it up with the warden--" I didn't get one more step past the table before his left hand circled around my wrist.

He pulled me in towards him, our eyes locking on each other. Not a word was uttered between us, he wrapped his arm around my waist. *I'm so close to him, I can smell his scent. His hand is warmer and softer than I expected.*

Oh god, I've wanted this so badly.

I knew it was wrong, that I should pull

away, but I didn't want to stop him.

His body shifted slightly in his chair, he was still restrained by the chains. My stomach filled with knots, my arms hung lifeless, unsure of what to do.

Without clear thought I stepped over the chain that divided our bodies. I broke the barrier that shielded us.

I stood between him and the table, our gaze fixated on each other. His right hand slid from below my knee and up my thigh. Firmly, he grabbed my ass then proceeded up. He continued to follow the curves of my body over my hips. A finger traced the outline of my breast and stopped at my neck.

Keep going, don't stop.

I became malleable in his hands. I wanted this more than I had realized. It felt right, a desire worth fulfilling. I couldn't stop myself anymore.

His forearms were strong, I could see

the detail of his tattoos; a colorful image of a large grandfather clock with elegant curved edges across the top, the gold in the hands appeared to glimmer under the light. There was script that wrapped around the sides and across the front that read, “Time heals everything.” It was beautiful.

I continued to touch his muscular arms, my fingers gripped them firmly as our breathing became heavier. He stared into my eyes while his hand stretched as far as it could go with the chains.

With force he entangled his fingers in my hair and pulled me down onto his lap. Our foreheads touched while neither of us released a blink.

The intensity of his stare sent goosebumps across my skin. His hand rested around my waist, the other gripped my hair tighter, pulling our faces closer together. The warmth of his breath spread across my cheeks.

My heart raced as his lips parted, not saying a single word.

His eyes and hands say enough. I know what he wants.

And I know what I need.

My skirt rose to the point were my panties became just visible to his sight. My legs straddled his as he pushed his hips closer towards me. I could feel the bulge beneath his prison suit push against my pussy.

He broke the silence with a hushed whisper. “Kiss me.”

I wrapped my arms around his neck and pressed my lips firmly against his. Our tongues intertwined wildly, stroking each other. A wave of elcctricity jolted through my body.

I'd wanted to feel him for so long, the sexual desire rushed over me. *How long has it been since he's had a real woman? He's holding me so tightly, I don't want him to let go.*

My panties became soaked as he gently rocked his lower body against mine. He pushed firmly under my chin to tilt my head back while he drew kisses down my throat. When his lips reached my collar bone he bit down gently. I was overcome by a sensation I had never felt before; a soft moan escaped me.

The guards. They're probably right outside the door. I want to moan loudly, yell for him to fuck me. But I can't. The need to be silent made the lust feel so much stronger.

My pussy dripped for him as my hips swayed back and forth against his enlarged cock. Even against the outside of his clothing, his hard shaft spread my lips apart. The extreme wetness dampened the orange fabric between us.

Owen lifted his arms up and tore my blouse open. He gripped my breasts in his hands, squeezed them firmly as he pressed his face between them. His prick grew harder beneath his clothes.

I wanted him, I needed to feel all of him deep inside me. I couldn't stop the animalistic behavior. My hand lowered to feel his erection, gently my fingers ran over it. It was as muscular as the rest of him. I could feel the outline of the tip as I reached the end.

I unbuttoned the lower part of his jumpsuit, exposing the flesh I yearned for. I gripped his pulsing, swollen shaft tightly in my hand and started to stroke it. Softly I raised my hand up and down, picking up the pace as his head went back and he moaned with ecstasy.

His hands clutched my hips as I pumped his length. I could see the rapture spread across his body. I couldn't wait anymore, I had to have him.

His eyes fell back on mine as I lifted my skirt above my hips. He peered down at my light pink lace panties. I pulled them to the side to reveal my slippery inner thighs. Reaching out, he ran a single finger down the thin trail of hair that lead to my lower lips.

Fucking hell, I can't take this! A moan escaped me as he continued tracing my slick pussy, his thumb grazing my clit. When I whimpered, Owen chuckled wickedly.

With his other hand digging into my ass cheeks, he plunged his fingers deep inside of me. Struggling to remain silent, I covered my mouth, biting my lip so hard I worried I'd leave a bruise.

I was on edge, burning from my toes to my eyes, a live wire. What the hell was I doing?

And why did it have to feel so fantastic?

My body arched as I rode his hand. I stroked him faster, his cock more rigid than steel. Owen curled his fingers, petting my inner walls as I crushed down on him helplessly. There was a chance, I realized with some excitement, that I could cum right here—before he even got his cock inside of me.

But it wasn't to be. Before I could tip over into an orgasm, he slid his hand away from my thighs. My pussy squeezed, arguing, desperate to keep him inside.

He brought his dripping fingers to his mouth and sucked the shiny surface. “Mmm,” he moaned, looking me dead in the eye as he indulged in my juices.

His boldness, this overt sexual side of him, had my belly flipping. Pure desire made me shift in his lap. When I did, the thick tip of his shaft rubbed my inner thigh. The heat of it broke me.

It didn't matter that he was a convict, or that I was his therapist, or even that neither of us had even mentioned or asked about condoms or birth control.

Any thoughts about protecting myself melted away.

I can't take this anymore, I'm done waiting!

I gazed into his eyes as I lifted my body slightly, guiding him towards my wetness. Had I ever had a cock so big inside of me? No, I didn't think so—and I had a deep, primal realization that it might be a challenge.

But I was soaked, my body buzzing from anticipation. His fat cock stretched me as he slid inside, burrowing further and further until I was seeing stars. How much of him was there? I imagined that single, initial stroke never ending.

Owen had other plans.

He thrust himself deep, the furry base of his shaft bumping my thighs. Biting my tongue, I thrilled at the sensation of being so full. His arms pulled my hips down harder with each thrust. The chains clanked loudly against the arms of the chair, but I didn't care.

His hands came up, reaching for my bra. I beat him there, unclasping it in one smooth motion. Owen narrowed his eyes at me, wordless appreciation all over his face. *He likes that I took my bra off for him.* The fact that I'd pleased him gave me a strange little thrill.

Leaning close, he ran his tongue across my hard nipples. They were stiff, easy targets for him. He circled the dusky areoles, teeth threatening to hurt me as he nibbled—but he never went too far.

I won't lie, I kind of wanted him to go further. This was a man who could tear me apart, smash me to bits. He had all the power, the advantage, that he needed. A beast like him, inked and massive, shouldn't have been anything but violent.

The potential for danger excited me... was that why I was doing this?

Stop thinking, I told myself, riding his cock as it flexed. *You've gone this far.*

Confined to his seat he thrust his pelvis upward, using every bit of inertia he could get. Our heavy breathing was the only noise that surrounded us. No words, no whispers, we just moaned like animals in heat.

His hands moved over my ass and gripped it firmly, fingers cutting into my flesh with the first real roughness he'd shown. It made me think about what he could do to me if he weren't chained up. Then, his mouth came closer, biting my collar bone frantically.

That was all I needed to crest the edge of climax.

Gasping, my voice strained as I locked up, muscles tingling. Pressure rolled through my lower belly, my pussy squeezing deliciously over his throbbing cock. I came violently, my nails clutching his shoulders like a vice.

Owen hissed through his teeth, arms curling around to bury me in his broad chest. While I was still twitching, I felt his cock thickening inside of me.

Is he going to finish without pulling out? Shit, we can't... we shouldn't risk that!

I knew it was an awful idea. *All* of this was a fucking awful idea.

But I never once tried to end it.

Holding me close, stealing my air, Owen went completely solid. Warm heat exploded in my pussy, his cum pumping again and again. It had happened—fucking hell, it had happened.

I'd let a killer cum inside of me.

His thrusts slowed, his cock pulsating as he leaned his head against my chest with a shuddering moan. Both of us sat in silence. Our skin had turned a warm, flushed red. Small beads of sweat trailed down his temples. Unable to move, we rested against each other. No words could form on my tongue.

The explosion of passion had been so intense I felt it in my bones. The tension had been building since the first time I had laid eyes on him.

I didn't care that what I had just done was wrong. I'd *needed* him.

Will my lust cool now? Can I move on and stop obsessing over this guy?

I had no idea... I didn't even know if I wanted that. I *should* have wanted that, but...

Glancing at the clock, I realized the guards would be here to remove Owen any second.

Shit. We can't get caught like this! Pushing onto his arms, I untangled myself from his grip. He released me, though I swear it was with some reluctance. Wincing, I slid off of his still rigid erection. I couldn't meet his eyes, I wasn't ready for that, so I turned away.

Fixing my clothing, I ran into the bathroom to get rid of any evidence of what we'd done. From the corner of my eye in the mirror I could see him, a smirk spreading across his face while he buttoned his prison wear.

I wonder how he feels about what we just did. Was it what he'd wanted?

The doorknob turned heavily and it startled me out of my thoughts. A muffle of voices could be heard outside, they grew louder when they realized the room was inaccessible to them.

"Yes, I'm coming!" I shouted. Briskly, I walked to the door. I took a deep breath and glanced back at Owen. His eyes peered at me as he ran his uninjured hand over his hair. One wink escaped his eye as he sat in silence. The grin on his face was so strong, I thought it would never vanish.

"Ms. Laroche! Open the door!" The pounding continued against the steel.

"I am! Hold on!" I clicked the latch and the door flew open. I was practically thrown off my feet. "Whoa! Easy guys!" I yelled as I stumbled back. "Everything is fine."

One of the guards stepped forward, glaring at me accusingly. "Why was that door locked? You aren't supposed to do that unless it's an emergency!" Small drops of spit sprayed across my skin as he yelled.

I wiped my cheeks and leaned in to read his name badge. "Thomas, I know it's for emergencies. Thank you. But I certainly wasn't allowing one of you over grown boys to walk in here during our session." I knew I was probably going to get in a *lot* of trouble for this move, and I didn't care.

Thomas narrowed his eyes at me before storming over to Owen. Together, the two guards tore him from his seat to remove him.

He didn't fight, he went along without a hint of struggle. Glancing back at me, he gave me a knowing smile. "Maybe I'll see you around." Then he was gone, escorted away.

The second I was alone, I began to pace my room. I couldn't stop looking in the direction of his seat. *I can't believe that just happened.* Slowing down, I froze as a new, terrifying idea hit me. *What if he tells somebody?*

The adrenaline started to fade and my thoughts became clear. If he told anyone at all about this I could lose my job! God, no, I could be arrested!

I sat at my desk as the weight of what had just happened began to crush me.

Fuck. Fuck! Why did I do that? My head fell onto my arms across the desktop. I was shocked with my behavior and lack of control. *I just screwed a prisoner. What the hell did I do? What came over me?*

This is horrible.

I slept with a killer.

My mind began to run in circles. A whirlwind of emotions flooded my body. I'd just jeopardized my career, my reputation. The depth of what had occurred was unimaginable.

At least there was no evidence.

Wait.

Evidence?

My head shot up, hair flying over my eyes. *We didn't have any protection! Oh fuck! There was no condom, he could have an STD for all I know!*

Fuck, wait, what if I get...

Pregnant.

The reality of the situation began to sink in fast. My heart pounded, not from excitement, but from fear. I was sick to my stomach over my actions. My breathing became heavy and irregular, I wanted to cry. The repercussions of what had just happened were too much to process.

I wondered what Owen was feeling. Did he have the same thoughts, same regrets?

This is bad. This could be really, really bad. I sat up in my chair, my hands clenching my desk in shock.

Maybe he won't say anything, and maybe I won't get a disease or... or knocked up.

I need to calm down. Take a deep breath.

Owen wasn't going to say anything. Somehow, as I sat there and mulled it over, I just knew it. He wasn't the sort, he was silent about his past as it was. As far as people knowing what we'd done, I was safe, but...

But what if I get pregnant?

What if?

***

That moment stayed with me for the next week.

I relived it daily in every thought. The week seemed to be a blur after our encounter, I walked around the prison on eggshells.

Every interaction I had with the warden pushed my stomach into my throat. I anticipated him saying something to me about it, or just plain firing me. I breathed a sigh of relief after each and every meeting with him when nothing occurred.

By the following Friday my nervous behavior around him had faded some, our conversations flowed easier for me. The fear of my illicit sexual experience being brought to his attention had started to trail off.

Before I knew it, it was time for Owen's hearing. The day of his possible release was here. It was a huge event, something I'd been waiting for for weeks.

Of course, my alarm decided to not go off.

What the hell! Why today of all days?

Every light on my way to the court house seemed to be against me. I sat at the latest red light, trying to apply mascara in my small visor mirror. *Come on! Come on! Turn green already! I'm the only car at the light, why is it still red?*

I had to get to this hearing, I wanted to

be there to support Owen. I'd turned in my report the day before and really hoped it would help to free him. I wanted to see him get his second chance at life. He made a mistake, but I truly felt he had changed as a person.

The tires on my small sedan kicked up snow and dirt from the pavement as I finally pulled into the parking lot. I tore my bag from the passenger seat, jumping out of the car.

The large granite building seemed football fields away. My senses heightened as I reached the mass of stone steps that led to two sheer glass doors. It seemed no matter how fast my feet were going the double doors were out of reach.

Barely reaching the top, I spotted Warden Lynch as he exited. “Warden, sorry I'm late. I...”

“The hearing is over, Ms. Laroche, everyone is gone now. You really need to be more attentive to the time.”

My heart stopped, knees locking up. "What do you mean it's over? I thought it was set to start at nine-thirty? It's only ten of, it can't be done already."

"I'm sorry, but it is." He continued down the steps, whistling a tune I wasn't familiar with.

"Well what happened? Where is Owen?" I needed an answer. I had to know if he was set free or sent back to serve the rest of his days behind steel barred doors.

"He's gone. One lucky fellow I tell you. One lucky fellow." He twirled a set of keys over his finger while the song he hummed merged into his last word.

I stood motionless as the warden walked past me. I expected to be happy and excited for Owen's new found freedom. Instead, deflation and disappointment took over.

I didn't get to see him. I missed my last chance to see Owen.

That moment to see his face when they told him he could leave was gone. What did he look like when he realized the cuffs and imprisonment that had been his life for years, was no more?

I don't know if I'll ever get to see him again.

I wondered where he would go, what he would do now. I wished I hadn't missed my chance to tell him good luck and congratulations.

The chance to get one last wink in my direction was over.

Chapter Eight

Charlie

Two months later

The key wouldn't open the deadbolt to the front door. I stood outside, shivering, jostling it from side to side. *Damn thing. I can't keep doing this everyday. Open all ready!*

The sound of a soft whimper filled my ears. "Hold on Biscuit, I'm coming."

I was frustrated with the frozen lock and gave it one last turn to the left, then heard a 'click.' *Finally*. A heavy sigh of relief floated out as I opened the door, the warmth from inside heating my face instantly. *It's time for a new lock.*

I dropped my purse to the wood floor and bent down to greet Biscuit. I'd adopted the dog that had been hit. After no one claimed him from the pound I was compelled to take him in. He needed me, the poor little thing would have been put down if I hadn't taken him.

There was no way I could let that happen.

"Hey lady! It only took you fifteen minutes to get in today. That's a record!" Sara yelled from the kitchen.

"Yeah, thanks for leaving me out there to freeze." A light chuckle escaped me. "Can we get a new one? This one sucks." I'd have bought one myself, but money was... tight. After my case with Owen had finished, the prison decided to let me go. Supposedly, they didn't need me anymore. Shock was the only feeling I'd had when the warden delivered the news to me.

He had called me into his office and said, "Ms. Laroche, I'm sorry to inform you but your time here is done. We appreciate the work you did and wish you luck on your next endeavor." Lynch had his feet up on the desk and was eating pistachios. He spit the shells into a small bowl on the floor.

A true professional, I had thought.

There had been no remorse in his voice towards me, he delivered the information with no feelings. It was as if we had sat down to discuss what he should have for lunch.

My spirit completely sunk in that moment. I had moved up here thinking this prison was a permanent position.

Well, I was wrong.

He told me that I had only been brought on for that one case, that they didn't have the budget to support my salary, and that he would keep in me in mind for the future.

I knew the real motives behind my termination. I had disobeyed his orders, made him look like a fool to his crew and he certainly wasn't going to have that. I don't think he knew how to handle someone who didn't bend over backwards to kiss his ass.

I tried to be optimistic about moving on. It was hard, the economy was in a bit of a funk, jobs were scarce. I had put in five applications already to a few neighboring towns with no luck.

Thank god for Sara. If I didn't have her here I'd be boarding the next plane back to Louisiana.

I'm not ready to go home. I wanted to make this leap up north work, not be a failure on my resume.

Sara had offered to let me stay with her until I found another job. She had an extra room in her condo and was more than willing to help me out. Without any income I couldn't afford to stay anywhere else.

Her place was small, but cozy. The flamboyant New York attitude she had could be seen all over the place. There were large fake trees placed in the living room on either side of the television. She couldn't be bothered having to take the time to water and maintain real ones.

The walls were full of replicas in fine art. From a Picasso in the entryway to a Warhol in living room. Sara loved the finer things in life. I was just grateful for her hospitality.

What a turn my life has taken. Going from being on top of the world to the bottom of the barrel. I don't know what I'm going to do. I feel lost for the first time in my life.

"So, how's the job hunt going? Any call backs yet?" The sound of her knife hitting the cutting board echoed through the hall.

"Ah, I put in a few applications today. So we'll have to see. Fingers crossed." I picked up Biscuit and walked into the kitchen. It smelled amazing. Sara was a great therapist, and an even better cook.

The apartment was filled with the smell of homemade tomato sauce with meatballs.

Being Italian, she made seven course meals every night. I was fairly certain I had gained ten pounds since I moved in a month ago.

"Can you get him away from the table, he's cute and all but I don't want his hair ending up in our dinner. I added enough spices already." She let out her high pitched, raspy laugh while pointing at my new companion with her butcher knife.

"Yeah, yeah. Alright." I leaned over and placed him on the tiles of the kitchen floor. "What are you making? It smells delicious, I'm starving." I picked up a raw piece of potato and started munching on it.

"Really, Charlie? Raw potato? That's gross. You should at least let me cook it first."

"What? It's good."

"Have you always done that? Because honestly it's weird."

I laughed and shook my head. "So what are you making already?"

"Well, we have salad, pasta with meatballs, compliments of my grandmother and her famous secret recipe. Don't ask me about what's in it, because I won't tell you. Garlic bread, and I decided to use up these potatoes, so homemade chips for later."

I grabbed a second piece of potato and shoved it into my mouth. "Were they growing eyes and staring at you?"

"Basically. I can't believe you're eating them like that." She wrinkled her nose and stuck out her tongue, making a gag face. "So nasty, Charlie."

"You should try it, it's pretty good." My smile broadened and I grabbed a third.

Sara slapped my hand with the spoon she was about to stir the sauce with. "No more, you won't have room for dinner if you eat them all."

Since I'd been living here our friendship had grown so much stronger. I'd debated several times telling her about Owen and what had happened, but was afraid to let her in on my secret. I didn't want to be judged or scolded. But, I needed advice.

He'd been on my mind, now more than ever.

I wonder where he is, what he's doing. Does he ever think about me?

After losing my job it seemed the world had crumbled around me. At this point how much worse could things get?

"Hey Sara, there's something I want to talk to you about."

"Okay, shoot," she said.

"Um, I don't know how to start, actually. It's hard to explain." *I don't have to tell her everything. I could leave out some details about it. Maybe sugar coat it a bit. Some advice would be better than no advice. And technically, he's not a convict anymore, or my patient.* "Alright, so there was this guy that I was really really into…"

"Guy! You never mentioned a guy to me before! Do tell," she said, resting her chin on her fist against the counter top.

I cringed at her enthusiasm. "I wasn't sure where it was going with him. But honestly, he's completely not the type of guy I would have ever pictured myself with."

"Where did you meet him? Is he cute? I can't believe you didn't tell me about him." She waved her spoon at me like a mother scolding her child.

"We met at work--"

"Work! Was he a guard? Some of those guards are so hot, with their uniforms and tight pants. Did you *sleep* with him?" Her eyes were large with curiosity. She loved to know the juicy information.

Sara had a good heart, great intentions, but her addiction to gossip drove me crazy. She was the person who had the subscription to every tabloid magazine. She knew everything about peoples' personal lives, from politicians to the clerk at the local grocery store. Who, by the way, I now knew slept with the manager for a larger discount in the store.

I knew more about the lives of those around us than they probably knew about themselves.

My eyes rolled from her bombardment of questions. “Anyway, I'm just having a hard time. He is constantly on my mind. I've debated possibly trying to find him. But I don't know, maybe I shouldn't. He's not exactly the dating type.”

“You avoided my question. Did you sleep with him?” Sara placed her hands on her hips, eyes glaring at me for an answer.

“Yes,” I muttered out. I couldn't bring my gaze to hers. I fixed them upon Biscuit who was so elegantly cleaning himself in the corner.

“So, you slept with this guy and haven't

heard from him in a while? Sounds to me like he just used you. I hate to be the bearer of bad news, but I wouldn't be wondering about an asshole like that."

"It didn't happen exactly like that. I don't feel used." I grabbed an uncooked piece of spaghetti.

"You better not be thinking about eating that raw, too! What are you, pregnant?" She laughed and turned to tend to her sauce.

Pregnant? The question made me stand straighter. *No. No way. I had my period last month. It was much lighter than usual and didn't last as long as it typically would, but I still had it.* There was a lot of stress lately. I assumed that contributed to my abnormal cycle.

My eyes peered down at the spaghetti I had begun to eat. *Why am I eating this? I don't remember ever wanting to eat raw pasta.* I ate weird things occasionally, but still...

No, it's not possible.

It'd been two months since I had sex with Owen.

Silence filled the kitchen, Sara glanced my way. “Look, I'm sorry. It's just that I've been there before. Don't let it get to you, there is always someone else. He probably isn't worth it, especially if he hasn't called you.” Her voice was sincere and her eyes full of concern. “He must have been good in the sack for you to still be thinking about him.”

“It's not that, it's just he had been in a hard spot, now I'm in one, too. I guess I'm just curious about where he is now and what he's done with himself.” Nausea began to fill my stomach, I had the sudden urge to throw up. I tried to take a deep breath and suppress the feeling.

What is going on with me? Where is this coming from?

“You alright, Charlie?” she asked.

"Yeah, I'm fine. I just feel sick all of a sudden."

"Maybe it was the raw potatoes you just stuffed your face with. I would want to puke, too." Her face mimicked vomiting.

"Ha. Ha. Funny," I said.

Something is wrong, though. And I have felt different recently. I've been emotional, eating strange things, but couldn't that be from the stress of job hunting?

The cold nose of my dog against my ankle broke my train of thought. I leaned down and pet him on his head, quickly he flopped over so I could scratch his belly. His tongue hung freely from his mouth while his leg beat up and down.

"You're such a good dog, my little guy."

"You better wash your hands after that, dinner is almost ready."

"Yes, mom," I said as we both giggled. I made my way down the hall towards the bathroom. Another wave of unease hit me, making my tongue tingle. *Oh no.* I knew this sensation.

Holding my stomach, I swayed towards the door. As the bathroom grew closer so did my urge to throw up. I couldn't push it away. *I'm going to puke. What the hell? I must be getting sick, caught some type of bug.* Before I could fathom another thought my face was buried in the toilet.

“Charlie! You alright?” The sound of feet came thudding down the hall.

Gripping the edge of the toilet, I groaned. “Yeah, I must have caught a bug or something. I'm just going to go lay down for a bit.”

“You sure you're not pregnant? I've never seen you this color before.”

My eyebrows arched in disbelief to her question. “No, Sara, I'm not pregnant.”

Sara rolled her eyes. “Alright, I'll let you

know when dinner is done and if you're feeling better, come eat. Otherwise get some rest. Hopefully it's just a twenty-four hour thing."

I shook my head yes and made my way to my bed. I flopped down on the mattress, feeling more nauseous than I could ever remember.

This is awful. My stomach is turning and I don't know why. I closed my eyes, hoping the spinning feeling would go away. A hand rested on my belly, the other across my forehead.

What if I am pregnant? A heaviness engulfed my chest. Panic started to set in.

No, I can't be. Stop it, Charlie. You're not pregnant. I could hear my heart pounding out of fear. What would I do? I didn't have a job or a stable home, and no clue about kids. The thought of carrying a child and raising it alone scared me.

I could always move home. I'm sure

my family would be there for me. Gritting my jaw, I took a slow inhale of air. *I'm not pregnant. I can't think like this, I'm getting all worked up for no reason. This is crazy.*

My eyes opened to the brightness of light. Sleep had taken over while I laid in bed resting. My arms stretched up and it felt good. Biscuit rested at the foot of my bed as he always did.

As I looked at him I thought back to how lucky he was to be alive. It was great for me to have him and know he was safe.

I wish I knew if Owen was safe.

Suddenly Biscuit lifted his head, his ears leaning forward. A soft knock resounded against my door. He knew someone was there before they made themselves known. A quiet bark released under his breath.

The door opened slowly and Sara poked her head in. "Hey, good you're awake. How you feeling? Any better?" she asked.

"Yeah, I think so. No nausea yet." I gave her two thumbs up and a smile.

"Good, I have to head out for a few hours, you need anything?" she asked.

"No, I'm all set. But, thanks." I pulled the covers up and reached for the remote. "I'm just going to lay here for a bit. Wait for my new employer to call and beg for me." I glanced at my cell phone on the nightstand.

She smiled and nodded her head up towards the ceiling. "Excellent. Well, call me if you do."

I heard the front door close. "Just you and me, Biscuit." His tail wagged as a rumble spread across my stomach.

I'm starving.

The wood flooring to the kitchen was cold against my bare feet. I opened the fridge and looked in. W*hat to have?*

Eggs and toast. That would be perfect.

The smell of breakfast started to

permeate through the condo. The idea sounded delicious, but as the food began to cook nausea set in again.

Come on! Really? I have to be coming down with something. The hunger disappeared and all I wanted to do was throw up. The smell of the food cooking caused my insides to turn.

Could this be morning sickness? I've never experienced this before, no matter how ill I was. It's different. Maybe I should just take a test to ease my nerves.

I will, that will stop these stupid thoughts. Damn Sara and her comment.

The drug store was just a five minute drive up the road. I entered and made my way over to the family planning section.

There are so many! I don't know which one to use. It was mind boggling, the number of different choices there were for pregnancy tests.

I shut my eyes and chose the first box

my hand landed on. It was a pink box, decorated with flowers and butterflies. *Is all that necessary? Seems a bit extravagant to find out about being knocked up.*

It doesn't really matter, I'm not pregnant.

At the register my hands trembled. The cashier, an older woman about sixty, smiled while she rang up the item. "Is this all?" she questioned, I could tell she wanted to ask more.

"Yup, that's it." My eyes darted around behind her. *Please don't ask me anything else.*

She peered at my hands as I handed her the ten dollar bill. "Nervous, huh?" I stood speechless, not sure how to respond. "Well don't be, no matter how it turns out, everything works out in the end." She winked and passed me the bag. "Good luck."

"Thanks." Swiftly I pushed the bag into my purse and walked back to my car. I glanced around the parking lot with the hope I wouldn't run into someone I knew. The door slammed loudly and I rested both hands on the steering wheel, a deep breath escaped as I squeezed the rubber tightly.

A heaviness pressed down on my entire body, enough to physically shift my shoulders forward. *I can't believe this. What if I am? Oh god! What if?*

My head fell onto my hands. *Calm down, slow breaths. You're not, this is only for assurance.* I shifted the gear into drive. *Let's go and get this over with. You'll feel better once it comes back negative.*

Back at the condo I braced the box in my hands. I spoke out loud to myself. “Alright, let's just do this. You're not pregnant. So, piss on the stick and be done with it.”

My body shook from nerves, each muscle quivered individually. *Why am I so worried? I know I had my period last month. Just ease my mind to be sure, it's not a big deal. It's going to be negative anyway.*

I couldn't stop my fingers from shaking as I opened the directions. Carefully I made sure to read them all. I wanted to do this right and not end up with a false positive. It seemed simple, fool proof even.

All that needed to happen was for me to pee on the hormone detector, let it rest for three minutes, and if there was one line then it was negative, two lines positive.

Here we go.

Those three minutes were the longest I had ever experienced. I was sure I'd made a track around my room while pacing, waiting for my cell phone timer to beep. Biscuit followed me around in circles as if we were playing a game, his tail wagged from side to side with delight.

It's not going to be positive. No way it's positive.

Yes, the last time was unprotected. But,

it's been a while now. I think I would have felt symptoms sooner.

And I had my period! I had it.

It's negative. Absolutely negative.

Startled out of the self talk by the beeping of my phone, I glanced down at my dog. “Alright, ready for this?”

Biscuit just stared back happily, his tongue hung out slightly as he tilted his head to my question.

I inhaled a deep breath and slowly walked towards the bathroom. The image of an inmate walking to death row crossed my mind; that lonely trek down a dark corridor to a deadly finale.

My heart raced as I approached the doorway. I didn't want to look down, I wouldn't let myself. My eyes closed while I stood over the sink where the test rested.

Just look down. Don't be scared, it's negative. Negative.

I forced one eye slightly open and glanced down.

Two lines.

Positive.

Chapter Nine

Owen

I glanced down at the watch on my wrist. *Two hours left,* I thought as I stared at the undercarriage of a rusty, wood paneled wagon. *What a piece of shit.*

Life outside the walls was a tough adjustment. Time had stood still for me, while the surrounding world changed at a rapid pace. Everything seemed more difficult than I remembered.

But when you go from a life of crime to the straight and narrow, it should be expected.

I could make one call and be free of all this shit. It would be so easy for me to dial a few old friends. I just don't want to end up back at that place.

I wasn't used to all this freedom. Flash backs hit when the buzzing of my alarm goes off each morning. For a quick moment I'd have to catch my bearings. Recognition needed to set in that I was no longer confined, that the bell was a clock and not the jail house timer.

Sweat dripped down my temple. I wiped it away, smearing grease across my cheek. That mere trickle of water brought Charlie into my mind. That last meeting with her, our bodies hot and wet...

It was unforgettable.

I wish I could feel her again. The moment she slid herself down over my cock and how her body arched with pleasure, the smoothness of her skin against mine had stayed with me.

I hadn't stopped envisioning her. When the smell of exhaust fumes burned my nostrils,

I replaced it with her scent. A southern accent caused my head to turn.

I need her again.

There was one day in the supermarket when I thought I'd had seen her. Dark burgundy hair flowed over the woman's shoulders, she had the same hour glass figure from behind.

Except it wasn't her.

That split second of excitement vanished when she turned around. An unrecognizable face glanced my way.

Before that instant, I had almost placed my lips to her ear to whisper, “Did you miss me?” Thank god I'd held off, it would have landed me back in prison. A sexual harassment complaint would not go over well with my parole.

“Hey! How you making out down there? You napping? Let's go! Adjust the suspension bolts already,” Bill, my boss, yelled. He was a tall, hefty man with a hot temper.

Owner and manager of 'Monroe's Mechanics,' he had been hiring released convicts for years through the prison employment program. It worked for both of us; I got a job and he got a major tax break.

He was good to me though, and I was thankful for that. He didn't treat me any differently than the rest of the other guys here. I liked him, he had a good sense of humor, but no problem telling someone where to shove it; a fair man, who wanted the work done quick and right.

“Yeah! I'm on it!” I gripped the ratchet tightly and turned. “Fuck!” I grunted as my hand slipped off and hit the sharp metal edge, slicing the top open.

“What? Did you fuck up something?” he asked.

“Yeah, my hand.” I rolled out from underneath, displaying the gash I had just received.

He crinkled his brow. “What do you want me to do? Kiss it and tell you it's all better? Go bandage it up and finish the job. No worker's comp complaint either, it's just a scratch.” He let out a hearty laugh, his beer belly rattling up and down with each breath as he slapped the top of the car and walked back to his office.

I shook my head as I stood. *Always worried about getting sued.* I made my way through the car parts and tools spread across the floor. The shop had just enough room to work on two cars at a time. Any of the empty space was strewn with random items, broken and new. Each step I took I had to avoid some object in my path.

Bill doesn't want any worker's comp, yet he let's this place look like a hoarder lives here. I chuckled to myself on the way to the sink.

The water stung as it ran over the fresh wound. My eyes squinted in pain while I tried to remove as much of the grease as possible. I started to remember how my hands had been the last time I saw Charlie, all bandaged and swollen.

I didn't feel any pain that day. I only felt her.

All of her.

"Hey, Owen! What are you deaf now, too?" Bill's voice crashed into my head.

"What?" I responded, slightly dazed.

"I've been talking to you and you've just been staring at the water. It's not that bad man, I think you'll live." He patted my shoulder and smiled. "I'm leaving for the night. Finish up what you can and the rest can be done tomorrow. Don't forget to lock up when you go." He started to walk away. "Oh, and I just got a call from Sammy's tow. They're bringing in a car that broke down, after that you can head out."

"Sure thing." I liked that he trusted me enough to let me close down the shop. I'd been trying hard to stay clear of any trouble. *All those robberies and bad decisions, they got me no where. I'm glad I haven't heard from Brice. I want no part of that world.*

For a short time I wondered if my brother would try to find me. The day of my release had been plastered all over the papers. Weeks after, I still looked over my shoulder, anticipating his crooked grin.

I attached the bandage to my hand and made my way back under the wagon. *Why do people want to dump money into a shit box like this?*

The next forty minutes were spent gazing at the dirty mess above me.

Where the hell is that tow truck? I'm ready to go home, shower, and eat something. I hate waiting around for these fucking guys.

They go at their own pace.

Light flooded the garage and the sound of tires against the gravel parking lot echoed through the room. I pushed myself out from underneath the car, pulling the rag from my back pocket. I wiped away the grime on my hands, ready to give the tow-driver an ear full.

Don't be a dick, Owen. If I rag on this guy Bill will send me packing. I need this job, I don't want to end up in a ditch. I tilted my head against each shoulder to crack my neck. *You know what, fuck it. This guy needs to know people aren't going to wait around for him. I don't need to be a complete prick. Just a little kick in the ass might help.*

I walked to the service door and threw it open. "It's about goddamn time! Did you get lost or something? You realize I can't sit around waiting for your lazy ass to stroll by when you're finally ready to do your job, right?" I waved the rag as I approached the driver's door.

The headlights blinded my vision of the truck. My eyes moved sidelong in an attempt to see the man behind the wheel; the door flew open. “Yeah, sorry about that man. I needed to stop off briefly for this young lady.” His voice was scratchy, as if he had smoked two packs a day for the past twenty years.

I stopped in my tracks, my legs as heavy as cement. The passenger door opened slowly. In the darkness of night a silhouette emerged, her face shielded in shadows against the glare of luminescent bulbs.

I brought my hand across my forehead to ease the brightness.

Is that...

No. It can't be.

My heart pounded in my chest as I squinted to get a better view of her face. I felt my lungs constricting, stealing any sound I could have made.

"Owen? Is that you?" The southern tone was melodic in my ears. I stood in awe, confused and unsure if this was really happening.

So much of my time had been spent looking for her in the face of every woman I passed by.

After all of that, has she really been dropped on my doorstep?

I'd fantasized about running into Charlie and what I would say. In my daydream I would walk up quietly behind her, leaning in to place my hands around her waist. "Hello, beautiful," I'd whisper into her ear.

This was no daydream.

The only word I could find on my tongue was, "Charlie?"

Light broke across her figure as she stepped into it. Each curve of her body was enhanced by the radiant glow against the blackness behind her.

For the first time in my life, I couldn't speak. *She's hypnotic to my senses.* With just her presence, energy spilled into my body.

She looked at me, scanned me up and down. The centers of her glorious eyes shined, a million emotions I couldn't read. Was she happy to see me? Scared? I wanted to reach into her head and find the answers. Not knowing was painful.

Licking her lips, she said, “Hey, how are--”

The driver stepped forward, ending our reunion with his clipboard in hand. “I need you to sign this so I can get the hell home. It's cold as a witch's tit out here, man.”

I glared at him angrily for not letting her finish her sentence. Forcefully, I grabbed the form from his hand and scribbled my name. “There. Now you can go.”

He nodded, turning towards Charlie. “Are you all set, Miss? Do you need a ride home?" His words were polite, but the way he ogled her chest gave away his motives. There was no way I was going to let her ride home with this pervert staring at her tits the whole time.

"No," I growled. "*I'll* get her a ride home. You can be on your merry fucking way." I didn't know him, but I hated him. The way he looked at her filled me with anger. No one had a right to do that. This woman was mine, even if he had no clue.

Hell, even if *she* had no clue.

My fists balled up by my sides. *I want to knock this guy's fucking teeth down his throat.*

"Alright, man." The driver held his hands up in defeat and climbed back into his seat.

Looking over, I watched as the tension in Charlie's body vanished. Her shoulders slid down, away from her ears. Had the guy been creeping on her the whole ride? I itched to reach out and hold her, to comfort her.

As the red from the tail lights faded into the distance my eyes were drawn to hers. I knew she hadn't expected to see me here. Hell, maybe she hadn't expected to ever see me again.

Her hands rubbed together swiftly back and forth, the tip of her shoe twisted in the dirt. The silence between us stretched to the point of snapping.

I want to touch her to know she's real. My hand came forward, but at the last second, I ran it through my hair instead of brushing her pink cheek. “Come on inside,” I said, “It's cold out.” I gestured towards the door with a nod of my head.

She remained still, her feet motionless. I could see the uncertainty in her eyes.

I smiled and said, “Come on, I won't bite. Unless you want me to.” Winking in her direction, I headed for the garage.

Charlie hesitated, then followed me warily. This wasn't the confident, self-assured woman I'd met months ago. *She's keeping her distance. Is she afraid of me now that the cuffs are off?*

Or had something else happened?

I opened the door and with one arm guided her in front of me. “Ladies first.”

“Thanks,” she said, pausing at the door. Her eyes darted around wildly in every direction possible, except towards me.

Why is she being so different? I wondered. “Go on in, it's fine.”

Her body passed mine and I noticed how she turned her shoulder away to avoid brushing against me. “So this is where you work, huh?” Her large, green eyes glistened as they examined the space.

“No. I broke in to steal the car parts. You know, so I can sell them on the black market. This shirt with the name badge is just a diversion for any asshole tow truck guys." My grin went ear to ear.

A smile began to spread across her face. "Ah, I figured that. You can take the man out of the crime, but you can't take the crime out of the man."

There. That's a hint of the sharp edges she had before

"See, you did figure me out," I said. Propping my hands on my hips, I slid my thumbs into my belt loops. The action drew attention downwards, and I caught Charlie's eyes when they flicked to where my cock was tucked away.

Her cheeks blushed when she realized I'd noticed. Immediately she looked away, turned her eyes toward the mess around us.

Squinting, the edge of my lips twisted into a knowing smirk. *Guess she hasn't forgotten about what we did last.* I watched her walk around, grazing her hand over various items. “Be careful, my boss would be pissed if you got cut on something.” I stepped towards her, trying to close the gap between us.

Her face remained fixed on a table covered in wrenches and cans of oil. “So, how are you getting me home?” she asked. Her slender finger followed the curve along one of the tools.

She is so fucking sexy. Those fingers should be touching something else. I want to bend her over that tool bench and slam myself deep inside. I bit the side of my lip, the thought of making her scream had made me painfully hard.

“Well?” Her voice broke through my dirty thoughts.

“What? I'm sorry, I got distracted. Can you guess what I was thinking?” I grinned at her.

Charlie crossed her arms tightly. “You didn't answer my question. Which I'm not surprised, you like to avoid answers."

"Hey, therapy is done. I don't have to answer shit." Shrugging, I took a step closer to her. "Let me ask *you* something." My hand swayed out, gently twirling a strand of her hair around my finger. "Have you thought about me, Charlie? 'Cause I've thought about you." Her perfume radiated me, my nostrils flaring with my hunger.

"What are you doing, Owen?" Her tone was flat and annoyed.

It threw me off, but I simply dug my fingers deeper into her hair. *I know she wants this, too. I can feel it.* In the low lights, her mouth was puckered—tempting. *Those light pink lips give me chills. I'm going to kiss her, feel them against my face.*

She couldn't resist me before, and I won't let her start now.

I leaned in, but immediately her hand pressed against my chest. "Owen. We can't."

She turned her head to the side and spoke into the air. Her figure squeezed passed until she was an arm's distance away.

Staring after her, I tried to connect the dots. *Why can't we do this? Sure, this could get me fired if Bill found out. Shit, he'd be pissed just knowing I let her wander around, never mind if I had my way with her.*

But I don't care. I've spent to much time away from her. I need this.

I'm going to make her remember the fire we had.

Without hesitation I bridged the gap. My hand came up and gripped her chin, directing her eyes onto me. Even then, she wouldn't connect with mine.

She whispered, “Owen, I can't.” A soft breath released from her taunting lips. “It's just... I don't know.” Her head fell down towards the floor as she nudged a piece of debris with her foot.

The face I'd longed to see, the body I'd ached to feel, it was right there. But she didn't emit the same desire as she had in the past. *How can she be so unsure of what feels so right?*

Here we were, reunited after months apart. Our last encounter, Charlie had torn me to pieces, clawed against me in her need to have my cock deep inside of her.

She'd been the definition of wanton... obsessed.

And now she wanted to be coy?

No. I knew something was wrong, but as I stood beside her, taking in her slight breathing... the way her chest rose and fell... and the fact she hadn't run from me... I didn't care.

I didn't fucking care at all.

Charlie was *mine,* and that hadn't changed, no matter how long we'd been apart.

My arms reached around her waist to

pull her in. I pressed my lips firmly against the delicateness of hers, tasting her as she crumbled against me. The fight was gone, her walls were down.

In one fluid motion I shoved the junk on the table to the floor. Our lips never parted as I lifted her up, tongues remaining locked while her hands forcefully grabbed the back of my neck. The breaths that escaped us began to fog the small, cold window behind her.

"Owen," she whispered into my ear as her legs wrapped around my thighs to pull me closer.

"Still think you can't do this?" I asked. My rock solid cock pushed against the front of her jeans. Even through the thick material I could feel how warm she was.

Tossing her head, she knotted her eyebrows as if she were in pain. "Don't throw that in my face. I just..."

"Shh," I whispered against her throat.

“I'm not interested in explanations. The only thing I want to hear is you screaming my name as I make you cum over and over.”

In response, she shivered, holding me tighter.

I want to taste her.

My hands slid under the soft sweater that adorned her body. *Her skin is smooth as velvet.* All I wanted to do was kiss every piece of her as I lifted the clothing away.

“Touch me,” she hissed into my ear. Her hands dug into my back and pulled me down onto her newly exposed breasts. I didn't wait, I had no patience to draw this out.

My tongue twisted around her nipples, dancing up and down until they were shining. She gave a long moan, head falling back. I felt her skin warm with every lick. Her nipples hardened inside my mouth as I gently bit down.

This is what I've wanted. My hands ran

down her sides, over her hips, and firmly gripped the creases between her thighs and ass. "Have you been waiting for me? Is this what your dreams have been filled with?" My tongue ran over my lips while my finger tips slid across the edge of her pants.

Charlie dug her hands into my hair. Firmly she tugged as her head shook yes, biting down on her lower lip.

I can't wait to fill my mouth with her sweetness.

The jeans she wore slid off easily. A pair of blue lace panties was all that kept my face from tasting her pussy. I pushed my face against them, felt the soaked fabric on my skin. Her scent made me dizzy, insatiable. Pulling her panties to the side I exposed her glistening, hot lips.

Her eyes boiled with desire. Grinning up at her, I nuzzled the inside of her leg. "You smell amazing." Lightly, I slid the tip of my tongue up her warm pink center. I felt her body tremble when I stroked her swollen clit. Her thighs squeezed the sides of my head, her hands dug into my hair and pulled.

"Mmm, yeah." Charlie's voice cut through the silence, traveling through me, setting my pulse on overdrive. The hair on the back of my neck stood on end.

She tastes incredible, I thought as I buried my tongue deeper inside. I pulled my cock out and stroked it. Her eyes fell, watching me. God, I loved having her looking while I jerked off; it made me grow even more.

"I've never tasted a pussy that was this delicious," I said. My teeth grazed along her skin, causing Charlie to twitch—then shove her hips against my mouth eagerly.

Juice flowed down over my chin from her soaked pussy. My tongue spun faster, rapidly I ran it up and down over her clit. Her angelic moans rang off the metal surrounding us.

Abruptly, Goosebumps emerged over her skin. *She's about to cum. Look at her move and squirm. Her legs are shaking.*

"Fuck, Owen! I'm so close, fuck, I...!" Our eyes locked and her body tightened as she screamed when the orgasm hit. Tremors rippled down her calves, sweat collecting in the dip between her breasts. Then she licked her lips, and I was finished.

I couldn't hold back, I'd done enough of that.

Standing tall, I pumped my painfully-stiff cock a few times. It didn't take much, the tingles spreading through my belly until I saw colors behind my closed eyes. "Get ready," I panted. Hunching forward, my pearly cum splashed over her stomach.

Jesus... that was something else. Dazed, I lifted my chin to watch Charlie. Her hand lifted to brush the hair back from my face. The beauty of her eyes filled me, and all I could do was smile.

It seemed like ages before either of us spoke. “Here,” I said with a chuckle, lifting the rag from my back pocket and extending it to her. “I know it's not ideal, but it's all I have for clean up.”

Her lips twisted, but there was no joy in them. “Owen. What are we doing?” She wiped away my remnants from her skin.

“Well, I just got to know you better,” I said, winking in her direction.

Carefully, she pushed me away. I almost didn't let her; the sensation of her palm, even through my shirt, had my cock flexing again. Climbing off the table, she tugged her pants upwards. For a moment, I had a view of her perfectly shaped ass.

“You know what I mean,” she said flatly. “Seriously, we can't do this.”

“Why can't we? Who's here to stop us?”

"Owen..."

"Shh, Charlie." I buttoned my jeans, adjusting my stiff prick into the most comfortable position I could manage. "There's something about you that I like. Something I can't explain, but I'm willing to spend some time with you to figure it out." Smirking, I smoothed my hair back. "I know I'm not exactly dating material." My eyes directed her towards the dirty, mechanic hands I held up. "But, let me take you out some time."

"I don't know, Owen. I was your therapist. *Everything* we've done has been wrong." She ran her hand through her hair, then brought her thumb to her mouth to bite the nail. "That day in the prison—it shouldn't have happened."

Something cold dug into my gut. *She thinks that shouldn't have happened?* I considered Charlie, judging her nervous energy. *No. She doesn't really think that.* "If it was a mistake, why repeat it?" I asked.

Charlie locked up, staring at me with guilt plain across her face.

When she said no more, I pushed on. "Look, you're *not* my therapist anymore, so just think about it." The wickedness in my smile was obvious. "Besides, you're going to have to come back and get your car. Seeing me a second time is inevitable."

She rocked on her heels, digesting my comment. "I don't know."

Without giving her a chance to react, I grabbed her hips and pulled her in close. "You do know. We both know you want to see me again, Charlie."

A low, hot breath passed across her plump lips. Even after we'd fooled around, the tension between us hadn't vanished. With nothing holding us apart, Charlie rolled her body closer to mine. Her need was constant, and it had mine burning like wildfire.

Watching me from under hooded eyelids, she mumbled, “I guess I could think about it.” Her thick lashes made her sideways glance look suspicious. “I have a lot of shit going on right now, and... well... never mind.”

It looked like she wanted to say something else, but she didn't.

Ignoring the flicker of confusion that rose in me, I grinned. “That's all I ask. So, you need a ride home? I could possibly--”

“Call me a taxi? Yes.” She smiled a little and laughed.

With some reluctance, I released her hips. I longed to dig my fingers into her sweet ass a second time, but not now. Something was off with Charlie, and I wanted to let things end on a high note. Pushing her wouldn't be helpful. “Alright, hang tight a moment.”

In the main office of the garage, I found the old land-line phone. The taxi company said they'd take twenty minutes to get here. That was definitely not long enough for me; I didn't want her to leave.

Deciding to take advantage of the wait, I sat with Charlie on the bench and chatted. It was small stuff, just keeping the air calm as I got to know more about the woman who'd plagued my dreams.

She told me about how she was let go from the prison and that after a botched interview a town over, her car shit the bed. So, needless to say, things had not been going her way.

The horn blared as the taxi approached. “Alright, there's my ride,” Charlie said. She looked just as disappointed as me. “You'll call when you know what's wrong with my car?”

“Yeah. That's usually how this works.”

I won't let her walk out that door forever. I lost her once and I'm not about to loose her again.

Awkwardly she stood in the door,

unsure if she should lean in for a hug. I didn't bat an eye, I wrapped my arm around the small of her back and pulled her in close. Before she could object I pushed my lips onto hers.

Charlie didn't resist. But how could she?

It had been a short time since we'd met, and even shorter since we'd reunited. Yet, the reality was this: Charlie was mine. I'd taken her, and I planned to extend my claim with each second she was by my side.

Charlie was mine. And I suppose, in a way...

I was hers.

Chapter Ten

Charlie

The ride to pick up my fixed car seemed long and endless.

It had only been a few days since I'd dropped it off at the garage. Days since I'd done the impossible.

I'd found Owen.

My nerves intensified the closer I came to seeing him again. *I can't believe this, of all the places in the world, he was right there.*

And I let myself get drawn back in!

The large, dirty sign that hung at the entrance to the auto shop came into view.

Alright, you can do this. Go in there, tell him "No." I couldn't date him! I just couldn't.

This baby was going to need stability and structure. Owen was a former convict, a man with a questionable future created from his own bad choices.

Not as if I've made the best choices, either.

I exhaled loudly. My hands ran over my thighs so quickly my jeans became hot from the friction. The driver of the taxi looked back at me in his rear view mirror, his stare expressionless.

I gave him an awkward smirk. *He's probably thinking you're nuts. Calm down.*

It was a challenge to do that. Hell, it was impossible. How would Owen react to me telling him that, in spite of what we'd done, I couldn't date him? Anger? Maybe, disbelief?

As I got out of the car my feet hit the ground like blocks of cement. The heart in my chest pounded like a bass drum, the deep sound radiating through my bones.

I still can't understand how quickly I gave in last time.

Why did I do that?

The moment I'd realized it was him, I'd

told myself to keep distant. But I couldn't. The strength to stand firm crumbled under his hands. His voice swept through my body with such force I couldn't resist him.

He was too magnetic. Just the thought of his hard torso, the curved, thick shape of his cock... it had me sweating.

The sound of an air gun buzzed from within the building, freeing my rambling mind. At the doorway I poked my head inside, not seeing a soul around. *Where did the noise come from?*

“Why, Hello there.” The deep, baritone voice floated over my shoulders.

Startled by Owen, I jumped slightly. “Hey! I, uh, didn't expect you there.” The corner of my lips fidgeted. *Settle down, deep breaths. He doesn't need to see you this stressed, he'll know you're hiding something.*

He stepped out from behind an old seventies conversion van. His face was spotted with streaks of grease, sweat dripped slowly over his temples. The material of his shirt stretched over his chest, every single muscle along his stomach shifting visibly.

Owen was a living Greek god.

Wow, had been the only thought in my mind. My gaze followed his broad shoulders to the partially unbuttoned shirt, some of his dark ink exposed. Images of a few nights prior rocked into my mind.

He's mesmerizing in so many ways. I adore the way he looks at me. His strong, yet gentle touch. I can't explain the hold he has over me.

“I'm pretty sure I mentioned last time that I worked here.” He laughed as he wiped the black smears from his knuckles.

My giggle was frantic. “Yes, I suppose you did.” Hating how I was acting, I looked around the room, eager to change the subject. “Anyway, what was wrong with my car?”

“It was nothing. Your alternator had froze, a little W-D forty did the trick.” His hand came up in a spraying motion. “Simple, no surprises.”

No surprises. Unlike me.

Since I'd found out, I'd wanted so badly to tell Owen what was making me so edgy.

I was carrying his child. But how did I give him that news?

The uncertainty of whether he would embrace happiness or show fear and resentment kept the words from forming on my tongue. The secret I held pressed on me constantly, crushing me into the floor so I couldn't find the strength to tell him the truth.

Not even now.

I was a coward.

Coughing into my fist, I nodded. “Alright, that's good news then. How much do I owe you?” My eyes glanced over towards the table we had used during our last encounter.

Owen followed in suit, a slow smile spread across his face. “A date. All you owe me is that.”

From the backroom across the shop, a voice rang out. “Owen! Are you harassing our customer?” A round, red faced man poked out from behind the open door.

“No, Bill.” Owen drew his hand over his hair and smiled in my direction, as if to say, “Here we go.”

“Well, stop jerking around and let her be on her way. I'm sure she has better things to do than shoot the shit with you. Not to mention the job *you* still need to finish.” His face disappeared as quickly as it entered.

Owen sighed, rubbing the side of his neck. “That's my boss. He gets a little antsy over the work here.”

“Yeah, I guess so.” I couldn't help but grin. Seeing Owen get barked at by a man who wasn't in law enforcement was surreal.

"Before he gets on my ass again, how about that date?" His forehead crinkled up with the question.

As much as I want to say yes, a piece of me is screaming no. "Owen, I don't think that's a good idea." I shoved my hands into my pockets and stared at the floor.

"Come on, it's not like I'm asking for a lot. And I do believe you just had free work done to your car. So, you sort of owe me," he said.

I stood silent for a moment. I had convinced myself to not take this date, the many reasons to say no ran through my skull. He was a man who had been lost and unstable most of his life. *How would I ever tell my child that his father is a killer, a murderer?*

Desperately I wanted my therapist mentality to take over, to talk me out of making a bad decision.

That voice never came. It fell quiet to the

raging feelings that consumed me entirely.

This could be my chance to tell him. The way he makes me feel inside is electric. No one has ever done that to me.

That has mean to something.

"Alright. One date." A sternness fell across my face. "But that's all I'm promising you. One date."

"I knew you'd say yes," he said with a tilted smirk.

"Don't flatter yourself too much. Maybe it's out of pity." He made it easy to play along, so I dove in, burying my unease in the flirting.

He looked up towards the ceiling and chuckled. "Yeah, I doubt that." His hand reached out and brushed my wrist, sliding the car key into my palm.

His touch gives me chills, those hands are delicate against my skin. He knows just how to use them.

"What time do you get off work?" I

asked.

He shifted his weight to one side. “I'm supposed to be here till six. Why? You too excited to wait?”

In a way, I am, I thought to myself. Playing with the key ring in my hand, I avoided his question. “I'll call you later and tell you where to meet me for dinner.”

“You'll tell *me* where to meet *you?*” Chuckling, he let his eyebrows crawl high up his forehead. “That's not how this works.”

I started to head for the door, tossing him a coy glance. “It is if you want to have dinner with me.”

Owen moved quick, blocking my path. From his pocket, he tugged out a shiny, black cell phone. “Hey, don't you need my number to call me?”

Flushing, I searched my purse. *Duh. Where is my mind at?* “Right, okay. Give me yours and I'll text you after.”

"How do I know you won't vanish again?"

"I didn't vanish," I said quickly. "I never meant..." I trailed off.

Owen eyed me, curious. "Never meant to what?"

"To miss your hearing," I finished quietly.

He stood there for a long while, his face expressionless. Then, he waved his phone. "Put my number in yours. I'll trust you to call me later for our date."

Relieved that he was dropping the issue, I started to type his number into my phone as he spoke it. "Okay, I'll see you later."

Owen flashed his tell-tale smirk. "One way or another, yeah. You will."

He really won't let me out of our date, will he? That fact made my heart swell. His determination was unlike anything I'd ever experienced.

On the way to my car, I peeked back over my shoulder. Owen stood watching me, his body resting against the wood frame. The heat in his eyes boiled, threatening to scald me if I stared too long.

As I drove off, his shape faded in the rear view mirror as the building blended into the trees behind me. The quiet of my car was disrupted by thoughts of concern.

How the hell did all this happen? I'm about to go on a date with Owen.

A convicted murderer.

A murderer that I've now slept with, gotten knocked up by, and then let him eat me out in a filthy garage.

Who the hell was I becoming?

Despite all my fears, a feeling of anticipation grew bigger. Owen made my body burn for him, melt with every stroke of his fingers. When we were in the same room, the atmosphere felt charged with his presence.

Could I just ignore all that? Refuse to acknowledge the sheer power between us?

The cold fact was that a baby had been placed in the middle of two people who'd lost their inhibitions and were taken over by lust. *Is that what I feel? Is this just surface level sex?*

It can't be, I've never felt like this before.

This is so much stronger.

Once home, I paced back and forth between my bed and the dresser, one hand resting on my stomach. The few outfits I still felt comfortable wearing were laid across the mattress.

Oh my god, I'm so nervous! What am I supposed to wear to this?

I picked up the one black dress I owned, my feet stopped in front of the mirror to hold it up. *I hope this camouflages my stomach.* The coldness of the silver glass brushed the tip of my nose as I leaned closer.

My eyes lowered to look at my belly. "What do you think?" I whispered to the growing life inside of me.

Biscuit appeared in the corner of my eye, tongue swaying back and forth. "Come on up." I clicked my fingers together as I plopped onto the bed.

The latch of the front door clicked, the walls shaking as someone entered the apartment. "Charlie? I've got great news!" Sara yelled.

I should talk to Sara. Tell her everything. I can't hide this secret anymore.

"I'm in here!" I tried to wipe the worry from my face. I didn't know how to even begin this conversation with her, and I wasn't sure if I was ready to.

Should I tell him first, before anyone else?

"Hey, guess what?" Her voice was full of excitement. She threw my door open and danced into the room.

I forced a curious look, but my thoughts were lost in the turmoil I faced. “What is it?” I asked, sounding more dull than I meant.

“There may be a position opening up at my office. I put your name in for it. Isn't that great?” Her smile was strong, hands curling up as she shook them excitedly side to side.

I tried to show some sign of excitement. “That's, that's good.” Desperately, I wanted to pull myself together.

She moved her eyes to the clothes laid out on my bed. “Ooh, does someone have plans for the evening?”

I shook my head yes, unable to speak.

“I just told you I most likely got you a job, and it looks to me like you're getting ready for a hot night on the town, so why are you acting like someone died? *What* is going on?” she asked as she sat down next to me.

I inhaled a rush of air. “Sara, you don't

understand. I'm going out with that guy I mentioned to you before."

Her hands fell to her lap. "And? Why is that such a bad thing?"

Here it is. This is my opening. If I didn't speak now, I might never tell her. Not until the baby was here, anyway.

My eyes rose to focus on Sara. Licking my lips, I wished I had some water. My tongue was so thick and heavy, I was sure no words would come out. In spite of this, I found myself talking—before I was even ready. "I'm pregnant."

"Oh my god." She stood and leaned against the bedroom wall, her hands clasping over her mouth as she inhaled a gulp of air. "Wow, you're pregnant! *Pregnant!* Whose baby is it?" I could hear the gossiper inside of her shining. My eyes shot her a glance, and immediately she understood. "It's *his?* The guy you crushed on at the prison?"

"Yeah, I haven't slept with anyone else." The magnitude of the situation made my body numb.

"How far along are you?" The normal brightness of her eyes disappeared. Concern had turned her skin ashen.

This is crazy! I can't even think straight. My eyes stared blankly into Sara's, I had no answer.

Her body lowered against the wall until she squatted across from me, her chin resting on her fists. "*Charlie*, what are you going to do?"

My mouth hung open, unsure of what to say. *What can I even do?* I fretted. *Telling Owen opens so many doors, but they could all lead to destruction.*

Ignoring him means risking being a mom all alone.

How can I fix this?

What the hell can I do to make this all

better?

I don't... I...

"Charlie!" Sara waved her hand in front of my face, pulling me from my thoughts. "Have you told him yet?"

I shook my head no. "I don't know if I want to."

"Why would you not?" Anger and worry filled her voice. "You have to," she said.

"I don't know if he's father material. His past isn't the smoothest, he's had a few bumps along the way. I need to think about the baby, too. What if I have this baby and he just walks out one day?" I still wasn't ready to tell her who 'He' actually was.

How do I tell this baby one day that their father is a killer, if I can't even tell Sara it's Owen's child?

"That's not up to you, Charlie. That's up to him. What he decides to do with this whole thing is on him. But you need to give him that chance. It's only right." She brought her arms up and crossed them over her chest. "Unless you're planning on a different option."

My eyes narrowed. "No. I could never."

"And you could never judge someone based on their past. I *know* you. Give him that chance. There was obviously something you liked about him."

When the words found their way in, it was the first bit of clarity I had felt in a while. A surge of excitement filled where panic had rested. My hand settled onto my stomach. *She's right, he deserves to know.*

I'm having Owen's baby.

I needed to give him that chance, the opportunity to be involved. I couldn't run from him, hiding from what fears lied within myself. It would be selfish to just out right deny this baby a father.

"Charlie, I'm not going to judge you. Regardless of your decision, you'll do what ends up being right," she said, laying her hand on my shoulder to comfort me.

A smile broke across my face. "Thanks, I need to finish getting ready."

Letting me go, Sara grabbed something off the bed. "One more thing." The black dress was tossed at me, covering my face and blinding me. "Wear this. You always looked good in black."

Minutes later I sat in the tub, the water hot against my skin. A bath always soothed my nerves.

I moved my hands through the water, parting the bubbles. Pieces of my blushed flesh shined under the lights. My head rested against the cool porcelain, a clear image of Owen's face fixed in my mind.

He's deeper than most people would guess. I doubt anyone gives him a chance to show that side of him.

He'd been closed off from the start, yet,

with time, he'd taken down fragments of his walls for me.

Owen was a man with a hard past...

But maybe a bright future.

And now we share a life.

The soft tap of my finger against the tub was exaggerated by the tile around me.

I knew what I had to do.

***

The dulcet tones of the violin drifted into my ears as I opened the tall glass door of the restaurant. The hostess area was lightly lit with candles adorning several small shelves against the back wall.

The floor, constructed of deep gray granite tiles, had a long floral runner ending at an elegant, handmade cherry podium.

I wonder if he's going to think this place is too fancy? I wanted to take him out of his element a bit. See if the refined nature here bothered him. He didn't object when I called him and said to meet me at Capriani's, one of the more expensive places in town.

That had to be a good sign.

My anxiety began to set in at full force. I had arrived a few minutes early, wanting to have some time to settle in and calm my nerves.

I can't believe I'm doing this! Dinner with Owen Jenkins, I never would have imagined this three months ago. A heavy breath pushed through my lips. I squeezed the small, red clutch in my hands and walked to the hostess.

A zealous smile spread across the young woman's face. “Hello, welcome to Capriani's. Your guest has been very eager for you to arrive.”

I looked at her, confused. “Wait, how do you know I'm here for someone in particular?”

There is no way he is here already. She must have me mistaken for someone else.

"I was given a very distinct description of who he was waiting for." She held a menu up against her face as she spoke. "It also helped that he's been checking the front every few minutes and saw you pull in. Follow me." Her smile never faded as she turned and entered the dining area.

My eyes studied the room, the candle light flickering brightly against the shiny leather of the booths. Each table was ornate with a tall vase filled with purple orchids. The cloth napkins resting on the tables were folded into the shape of birds, their color matched the flowers in the center.

As the hostess turned, I was struck by a sight I had never expected.

There Owen was, sitting in the booth, looking like one of the men in a GQ magazine. A black blazer rested over his muscular torso, a white t-shirt underneath tight against his skin. I could make out each crease of his abs under the cotton.

Oh my god. He looks incredible.

His gaze fixated on me as I was led to him. He didn't mute his overt appreciation for how I looked; he ate me up from feet to lips with his hungry stare.

He stood to greet me and my body began to warm, it was as if I had been out in the cold and was handed a hot drink. The heat poured over my insides, filling every space.

"Hello, beautiful. You look amazing," he said as he placed his hands around my wrists.

"Thank you." I didn't know what else to say.

I don't know if I'll be able to tell him about the baby. I need to, but this is going to be hard.

Just play it by ear. If it doesn't seem right, I won't tell him just yet.

"Sit. I told you before, I don't bite." He chuckled and led me into the booth.

Neither of us uttered a word for several seconds. I looked down at my place setting and began to fidget with the silverware. I couldn't make eye contact with him. My stomach twisted and turned in every direction.

I'm so ridiculously nervous! I want to vomit.

Get a hold of yourself!

"So," he said in a husky tone, "I'm going to be honest. I think you look so god damn sexy right now." He brought his finger up and brushed my hair behind my ear.

My face flushed bright red, briefly my eyes reached his then looked across the room. I knew he was going to feel my nervousness, sense that I was unsure and afraid of what I was doing.

Come on, Charlie, just say something. Anything.

The silence that coated my tongue evaporated. “Well, you don't look so shabby yourself.”

“I'd thought about just wearing my dirty work clothes. But, they didn't really match the shoes I wanted to wear.” He leaned back in his seat, the corners of his mouth raised up in amusement.

That single motion brought me back to the prison, our meetings. How sure of himself he had been and still was. *It's such a turn on to see him so confident.*

Before I could respond, the waiter walked up to our table bearing a full bottle of white wine. “Here you go, sir, our finest Chardonnay.” He lifted Owen's glass to pour it in. “Miss?”

“Oh. No thank you. Water will be just fine.” I darted my eyes between Owen and the waiter.

“What? No wine? This is a special

occasion, live a little." Owen lifted my glass to have it filled.

"No, really. I'm all set." I tried to remain natural. "Water is fine."

"Alright, so you're going to let me drink this whole bottle myself? Are you trying to get me wasted?" He wrinkled his forehead over my decline of the wine. "You want to take advantage of me, don't you?"

"Yes, exactly. You figured me out." I played into him a little. "I really want to get you so drunk I can do whatever I want to you."

I want to tell him the real reason I can't drink. I hated this game of lying.

Suddenly, I noticed his view was concentrated on the large window behind me. For that moment he was no longer present at our table. I turned to see what he had been looking it.

A large number of people, bundled up in winter gear, passed by. There seemed nothing unusual about the sight, but his eyes engulfed the dark figures on the sidewalk.

Why is he looking so intensely out the window? It's a busy street, that's all.

"You alright? What are you looking at?" Curiosity filled my voice.

He shook his head and took a large gulp from his glass. "Yeah, yeah. I'm fine. It's nothing. I thought... I thought I saw... never mind."

"Well then, tell me what you've been up to since you left Greene?" I asked.

For most of dinner, conversation was good. The scared feelings had lifted for a time. He talked about his job at the shop, and wanting to maybe open up his own one day. He shared that he had been trying to save to buy a house and really wanted to do things 'differently' now that he had a fresh start.

He seemed changed, more ambitious than I had expected.

Maybe he has turned a new leaf. He has goals and desires.

"Alright, enough about me. Tell me more about you. Anything good going on in the world of Charlie Laroche?"

I think I should just tell him. Say it and get it over with. Holding it in is killing me inside, he needs to know.

I have to tell him.

With all the talking I've done as a therapist, finding a way to tell him the most world changing aspect to both our lives was non-existent. I physically could not place the words.

What if he freaks out? I have no clue how he is going to react. The anxiety is actually hurting me inside. My chest is heavy and my entire body aches with fear.

"Yeah," I mumbled, "There are things going on. I may have a new job soon, which is great." I twisted my napkin in my hands. The sweat continued to form on my palms even with the cloth firmly gripped.

"Are you *still* nervous about being around me?" he teased. "See, a little wine would soothe that. And so would a massage from me." His grin was playful. "Here, have a sip of mine."

"No, really Owen, I can't." My left leg begin to shake rapidly.

"Look, I'm not trying to pressure you. I just want..."

"I'm pregnant." The words shot out across the table. For the first time that evening, my eyes remained frozen on his.

Shit, it just spilled out of my mouth.

Blankly, he stared at me. "What?" He looked lost, unsure of what he had heard.

"I'm pregnant." My mouth opened, shut, then opened again. "With your baby." I looked into his face for some reaction. I had to know what it would be, even if it was awful.

Owen's elbows rested on the table, he rubbed his forehead vigorously back and forth. His eyes were large, they drifted aimlessly around the room. Then, he leaned back forcefully into the booth, his arms flying up to cradle his neck.

What is he thinking? Maybe I shouldn't have told him? Was this a mistake?

Say something, anything! What is he going to do?

"You're pregnant?" he asked slowly. "For real, you're not kidding." Sitting there, he ran a palm over his jaw. "Fuck. Pregnant, I honestly didn't expect you to say that."

Alright, no yelling yet. He's still thinking, trying to understand this. Give him some time, let it set in.

His fingers spread on the table. Owen bent closer, the centers of his eyes as deep and liquid as a star-covered galaxy. He was an enigma, his emotions bottled away so no one could reach them.

I prepared myself for the worst. *Get ready to grab your stuff and leave. I don't want a a scene.*

What had I been thinking? Of course Owen didn't want to be a father. His life had just begun again, what sane person wanted the responsibility of a baby thrown at them, now, of all times?

He must hate me. I bet he's thinking I'm scum, or stupid, because I wasn't on birth control. But I wasn't planning on having sex! I didn't plan any of this! I...

“You know what this means?” he asked, tension low in his throat.

I said nothing, my hands balling in my lap as I waited for him to chew me out.

Owen blinked, a seriousness touching his hard-lined mouth. “This means our lives just became one. If you thought you could get rid of me before, good luck trying now.”

Every muscle in my body stiffened. “What?”

“You have my baby inside of you, Charlie.” Nothing in his face said he was joking around. He was flat, severe, eyebrows low over his eyes. “You're mine. That baby is mine. I'm not leaving your side, you're stuck with me.”

A ringing began in my ears. *He's really serious.*

I was his? God, why did that make me tingle?

He rested his head against his hands. “How long have you known?”

The seat squeaked as I shifted in place. “A few weeks now.” My body was tense, I had no idea what to expect from him.

“A few weeks? *Why didn't you tell me sooner?*” Frustration spilled from behind his gritted teeth, his fists rolling up into balls. I anticipated him hitting the table, pounding down on it as he had done during one of our sessions.

His hands are shaking, oh shit. What is he going to do? I didn't expect him to be upset over not telling him. "I don't know. I only ran into you a few days ago, and I was nervous about bringing it up." The muscles in my chest tightened, my breathing became quick and short.

His strong, muscular arms stretched out across the table, fingers linking on top of mine. "It doesn't matter, none of that fucking matters. From here, we go forward, okay? You get that?" His knuckles went white, almost causing me pain. Oddly, it was comforting. "Now, I'm a part of you forever. And you're a part of me. I'm not letting you go anywhere, Charlie. I'm going to be right here for that baby and you."

Frustration had been replaced by his primal nature. I fought the urge to kiss him. "Owen, I want you to be here for this baby. I do. But, are you going to be handle to this?"

I wanted him to say 'Yes,' to tell me he would do anything for this child. Worry clouded my beliefs. He was a felon, how did I truly know he wouldn't fall back into his ways?

His face twisted with seriousness. "I am *not* going anywhere. No matter how much you may want to push me away, that baby is mine. We're chained together, Charlie."

His fierceness made me shiver. *How can I feel such a desire?*

I should be worried, scared even, that he is the father of this baby.

But I'm not.

"Charlie, this baby is going to be the center of my life. And so are you. It doesn't matter what you thought about me before. You're carrying my family, my child, my blood." The playful eyes from when I arrived became solemn. He slid over next to me and rested his hand on my stomach. "This is my baby in here."

A single tear slid over my cheek. It made me happy to see him so accepting of the life inside of me. "It's our baby," I said, looking up at him. He brushed the tear away, bringing his face close, passionately pressing his lips to mine.

He says I belong to him.

Nothing had ever felt more right.

Chapter Eleven

Owen

The softness of her hair fell over my hand as I brushed it back from her shoulder. I was mesmerized by the glow of her skin. All I wanted to do was touch every inch of her flesh.

She's carrying my child. I never expected I'd ever be a father.

I couldn't stop staring at her as she drove us back to her apartment. The bottle of wine I had indulged in had hit me as we stood to leave the restaurant. Charlie wanted to take me home, but I'd insisted we needed to be together.

The ride was silent, we shared glances in the brightness of passing vehicles. I noticed her eyes twinkled under each set of lights.

I'm not going to be away from her. I'm going to keep her safe, be by her side every minute I can. She's not ever going to think she's doing this alone.

I'm right here.

And this is where I'm staying.

I leaned in close and drew delicate kisses down her neck. My hand glided down her arm and stopped over her belly. She turned to look at me, her face a tint of red under the stoplight.

I brought my hand around her cheek and pulled myself in to kiss her soft, silky lips. Sheer passion rained over my body. My cock began to grow, it pressed against my zipper. I moved her hand so she was rubbing over the bulge in my jeans.

She grabbed on firmly as I pushed my lower half up into her hold.

I would love to tear her from her seat and onto my lap.

Dammit, I have to fuck her.

Our passionate moment was cut short by the blaring of a horn from behind us. "Green light," I whispered under my breath.

“Yeah, I should probably pay attention.” Her giggle floated into my ears.

Even her laugh is sexy. God, the way her accent hits me makes every hair on my body twitch with excitement. We better be getting close or I'm going to explode.

“How much further? I'm ready to have you right here and now.” My hand reached up and squeezed her tit, slowly it glided down to her thigh.

“Down boy, we're here.” I glimpsed her smile under the street light as we turned into the parking lot.

The area was dark, all the condos were shadowed in blackness. It was late, not a single person appeared to stir in any of the other residences. The curtains were drawn on the apartment, only a faint light glowed above the front door.

“I'm sure my roommate Sara is sleeping. Keep it down when we go in.” She exited the car and waited for me to make it around to her side.

Her plump lips formed a smile when I grabbed her hand and walked beside her. It was freezing cold out, I stood anxiously, waiting for her to open the door.

"Sorry, this lock is horrible." She twisted the key repeatedly back and forth. "Shh," she whispered as the door slowly creaked open. I heard the sound of tiny clicks against the floor, followed by a tender bark.

"Biscuit! Shh!" she yelled within her whisper. The small dog ran wildly around my ankles, sniffing and jumping back with each step I made into the house.

"So, this is Biscuit. Cute ankle bitter." My words were soft and hushed.

Her arm came up and hit me gently in the chest. "Leave him alone. He may be small, but he's a trooper." She removed her heels in the entryway to quiet her feet. "Come on."

We walked stealthily down the hall to her room. Charlie flicked the light on and gingerly closed the door behind us.

Finally! I'm ready to rip her dress off.

“Here we are. Welcome to my humble abode.” She laughed and threw her purse onto the dresser.

“Yup, here we are.” My patience had run out. She stood facing the full length mirror at the end of her bed. I walked up behind her and wrapped one arm around her waist. My lips met her neck, I kissed the bare flesh intensely.

My other hand ran down her shoulder as her head fell back onto my chest. I watched her eyes close as her palm came up and gripped the back of my throat, her nails dragging across my skin.

This is what I've craved. All of her body, here to enjoy. No time limit, no restrictions.

Her scent drives me fucking crazy.

I'm going to make this a night she won't forget.

"I need you, Charlie." My words exited between kisses. "And you definitely need me."

Her eyes connected with mine. "I do need you. Both of us need you." She pulled my arm around to her stomach as she spoke.

My free hand began to unzip the back of her dress; it fell to the floor, exposing her angelic, white lace bra and panties. I could see the dark pink flesh of her nipples through the sheer material.

My cock grew firm beneath me. I savagely spun her around and pulled her in tight. I embraced her and my lips couldn't resist anymore. I kissed her intensely, our tongues intertwined in a dance of desire.

She pulled my jacket off my shoulders and lifted my shirt off. My body was damp from the heat between us.

Charlie ran her hands up over my chest,

crushing herself against me. “Take me, I'm yours,” she whispered.

I led her to the bed, but before I did anything, she reached down for my waist. Smoothly, she unbuttoned my pants. My erection pressed angrily against my boxers, making Charlie lick her lips.

Slipping around me, she laid back on her mattress. Her hands came up and touched her body, fingers delicately running over her nipples. Every curve moved and swayed, I watched her ache for me. She called me in with the motion of one finger.

All of that belongs to me. All her beauty is for me to indulge in.

I knelt above her on the bed. Her legs crossed and slid over each other, giving away her need. I unclasped the front of her bra. My fingers touched her breasts gently and I could see prickles form on her skin. She let out a quiet gasp as I continued my hand down.

The tip of my tongue teased her hard nipples. I swirled around each one, exhaling the warm air from my mouth onto her. She moaned softly with each pass of my tongue. Her head tilted to the side in pleasure and my eyes caught the ivory of her collar bone.

The sweet spot. If I bite it just right her pussy will drip for my cock.

My lips softly rode the entire length of her collar bone. Her hand came up and gripped the base of my neck, her fingers tugging on my hair. I bit down and she let out a loud, hot groan. I watched her shiver from the sensation.

"You like that, don't you?"

"Yeah." The one word left her mouth as she chewed on her lower lip.

I reached for her panties and her back arched off the bed. My hand ran down over the front of her lace coated mound. *She's soaked and dripping through them. God, I'm going to fuck her so hard.*

Her hand fell onto my cock, firmly she gripped and began to stroke. The harder she pulled the more solid I became.

"That's it, stroke my cock." I pushed myself into her hand as her palm reached the base. "You want to feel that? Feel that slide deep inside you?"

"Yes, I can't wait anymore!" She brought her hands up to squeeze her tits.

A woman who isn't afraid to touch herself is insanely hot, fuck.

I slid her panties off and spread her legs wide open. Under the light her pussy glistened with wetness. As I positioned myself above her, I felt her hand around my shaft. She took the tip and rubbed it delicately over her soaked velvet lips.

Her pussy was warm against my skin, I could feel my cock pulsing. She slowly guided me inside, her tightness sealing around me. The further in I pushed, the tighter she squeezed around my girth.

I felt her back lift from the bed, my hands sliding under to grab her ass. Squeezing tightly, I shoved myself in deeper. A high pitched moan escaped her mouth, her eyes fell closed and she wrapped her arms around me.

She's so wet. Her pussy is tighter than I remember. It feels so good being inside her again.

My cock penetrated her deeper and deeper. Every muscle tensed in my body with each thrust. I couldn't hold them back; The bed beneath us squeaked as our bodies collided wildly.

Her pussy grew wetter as my pace quickened. Effortlessly I slid in and out, my balls smacking against her ass as I drove myself in hard. Our bodies moved as one, her hips thrusting up as I pushed down.

“Harder! Harder!” she yelled into the air. “I'm going to cum, don't stop.”

This excited me beyond belief. Making a woman cum was empowering, better than my own orgasm, really. I ached to hear her lose control, straining as she vibrated beneath me.

Faster, I slid between her thighs. My cock was in her to the hilt, the delirious pleasure radiating from my lower belly and outwards.

I felt my balls tighten as we were both about to orgasm. Her loud moans turned to screams as she clawed against my back. I leaned in and bit down hard on her shoulder, pressing her into the blanket.

"Please," she begged me. "I'm so close, I..."

Guiding her speed with my palms on her ass, I chuckled in her ear. "I know how close you are, I can feel you milking me."

Her next whimper was enough for me. Hissing, I tossed my head, filling her with my seed as my climax rolled over me. My scalp was electric, nerves waking up until I was buzzing.

Charlie finished instantly, her pussy clenching on me while I still twitched with aftershocks.

Hanging my head, I backed up until my cock pulled free with a wet sound. Overcome by the erotic encounter, I fell limply onto the mattress. We laid beside each other, out of breath, glistening with sweat.

“That was fucking incredible,” I said between inhales. My head turn towards her and I motioned for her to come closer.

“Yeah, that was amazing.” She nestled her cheek into my chest as I wrapped my arm around her. She fit perfectly against me, a woman who'd been built to be at my side.

This was paradise.

“Charlie, you know I meant what I said earlier. You're not going to do this alone.” My eyes were sincere. I couldn't stop thinking about how I was going to give this baby everything I never had.

Especially an actual father.

My eyes opened to the smell of bacon. It took a moment to remember where I was. I felt the warmth of Charlie's body next to mine. *She is here, with me. It wasn't a dream. What a night, a hot memorable night. I'm laying here next to the mother of my child.*

Holy shit. My life is never going to be the same.

"Good morning," the delicate voice beside me whispered. She looked up into my eyes and buried herself closer. "Did you sleep alright?"

"I think that's the first time I actually slept comfortably in a really long time." I brought my lips down and kissed her forehead. She smiled as brightly as the sun through the window.

"I'm pretty sure Sara is up." She turned her head to the door and smelled the air. "You hungry?"

"I could be hungry. It smells delicious." I rubbed my hand over my chest as my stomach made a loud, angry gurgle.

"Well, I bet there is plenty. She's Italian, and only knows how to cook for no less than six." Her giggle was music to my ears.

As we walked down the hall I could hear bacon sizzling in the pan, mixed with the sound of classical music. I stepped into the kitchen and was hit by an array of aromas. Peppers and onions sauteed in one pan, mushrooms and garlic in another. It was a delicious overload to my senses.

A woman that I assumed was Sara stood facing the stove, steam pouring out from different areas in front of her. "Well, well, well," she said, "It seems to me like someone has a whole lot to dish to me this morning." She spoke to the room with her back turned. "I figured you were going to be dead to the world for a lot longer than this after what I…" Her words halted when she turned to see me standing next to Charlie. Her eyes were large with shock. She hadn't expected to see me.

"Good morning." I smirked and ran my hand through my hair.

"Oh, why hello," she said warily.

"Sara, this is Owen. Owen, Sara." Charlie's eyes darted back and forth between us uncomfortably.

I don't think she ever told her friend about me. Or at least she may have left out some info.

"Nice to meet you, Owen," Sara said. "You look familiar. Have we met before?"

She's probably seen me on the news. "I don't think so. But I've been on television a few times." I tried to stop myself from laughing. Charlie shot me a glance with a slight smirk.

Sara's eyes shifted between us. "Television? Uh huh," she said dubiously.

"Maybe that's it." Her sly squint ended on Charlie. "Alright, eat up you guys."

There was more than enough food, just like Charlie had said. Amazingly, Sara kept conversation light, never prodding about what I was doing in her home.

After breakfast I glanced down at my watch. "Shit. I need to go, I have to be at work in an hour. Charlie, I'm going to head out. I'll call you later tonight." I stood and brought my plate to the sink.

"I can give you a ride to your car." Charlie got up and started for her jacket.

"No, that's alright. It's just up the road a bit. I can walk. Go get some rest, it was a late night." My teeth glinted with my perverse joy.

Sara cleared her throat. "Do you guys need me to leave the room? Because I will. I don't mind."

"Sara! Stop. Alright, call me later." Charlie's face turned a bright red as she smiled and looked down.

I stepped forward and lifted her face with one finger. My eyes looked deep into hers as I leaned in and kissed her. “I *will* see you later, beautiful.”

She was speechless, but that was fine. It wasn't a real goodbye. I'd never say goodbye to the woman I was obsessed with.

As I walked towards my car, one thought warmed and comforted me.

My life has purpose now.

***

It was difficult for me to concentrate at work. I kept thinking about Charlie and the growing baby. My boss had already yelled at me a few times today because he'd found me just spacing off.

I'm not ready to tell anyone yet about what I learned last night. I want to figure everything out first. I need to make a plan, figure out what steps are next.

The next step has to be us moving in together. We'll need a place suitable to raise a baby.

A baby, that still has a weird sound to it.

I'm going to do this right.

Everything will work out.

I leaned into the engine of the minivan I had been assigned to work on. A simple job for today, replace the fan belt and radiator. Yet, with all the thoughts charging through my brain I couldn't focus long enough to even complete a full turn of my wrench.

I'm going to ask her tonight to move in with me. I know she's going to try and talk me into going slow, but how the hell could I do that?

She's having my baby! I need to have her with me.

No matter what it takes.

“Owen!” Bill screamed from behind me.

I lifted my head up quickly and hit the top of the hood. “What?” I yelled back while trying to rub the soreness away.

“Ha! That's what you get for being so god damn slow today. There's a guy looking for you out front. Don't take too long, and for god sake finish this already.” He rolled his eyes and briskly walked around the junk to his office.

Guy out front? Who would be here looking for me? I hope it's not a new parole officer doing a check in. They tended to change on me with no notice and no real reason at all. I'd had two different ones already since leaving the prison.

I grabbed my rag to wipe my hands and walked towards the front door. Through the small window a few feet away I could see a figure facing the street. I couldn't make out much since the glass had a film of dirt and dust that created a blurry, yellow hue.

When I reached the door the man remained turned away from me. “Can I help you?”

His body slowly rotated and his profile froze in my mind. That tall, lanky body with a head full of greasy dark brown hair, the tight lipped smile; it sent a wave of rage throughout my body.

Brice, what the fuck is he doing here?

“Hey, Owen, how you been? Long time no see.” He grinned the sleaziest smile ever with a mouth half full of teeth.

“What are you doing here?” I asked through gritted teeth. My hands began to shake slightly. *You shouldn't be here, why are you here?* The thoughts in my head began to race.

Just go back to the hole you crawled out of. I don't need you in my life, especially now.

“What? I can't see how my little brother

is doing? Ask you how things have been since you got out?" He walked towards me, his hands resting in the pockets of an old camouflage hunting jacket.

I didn't care what he wanted to ask. I just wanted him to disappear. "How did you find me?"

"Owen, come on man. You know I got resources. How was dinner last night?" He brought a hand up and lit a cigarette, inhaling a long pull and blowing the smoke in my direction.

It hit me in that moment, when he said those words, that it hadn't been my mind playing tricks on me last night. I *had* seen him outside the window of the restaurant. *Maybe all the other times I thought I'd seen him before were true, too.*

Has he been following me all along?

"Get the *fuck* out of here, Brice. I don't know why you're here and I don't care." I didn't want to yell at him, I was at work and Bill certainly wouldn't be happy if I got into a fight in front of the shop.

I turned to walk back inside, leave him where he was and forget that he had been here. I wanted no piece of what he represented. He was a memory from my past, one I had been trying to forget.

“Wait! Owen, look, I need your help, man. This shit is serious.” His eyes showed desperation. “Come on, this is life or death for me.”

I inhaled a deep breath, my fists curled, ready and wanting to hit him. “I don't care. You're on your own,” I spoke over my shoulder.

“Owen, I'm in deep. Way too deep. I got in with this gang, and... I owe a shit load of money to them. I just need you to help me this one time. That's it! Just this once.” His face filled with worry and fear, but I knew he was exaggerating to manipulate me.

"No. I'm done with all that shit. I've been done for a long time. Find another way to fix your issue." *Who the hell does he think he is? He leaves me for years. Ten years! Then he shows up and expects me to bend over backwards to get him out of trouble. No way! There is too much at stake for me now.*

I told myself I wasn't falling back.

And I won't.

"They're bad people, Owen. Really bad people. I can't do this alone. Remember everything I've done for you? Everything I did to keep you safe when we were kids?" Brice wanted to try and pull the guilt card on me.

Not this time, not anymore.

A dark laugh spilled from my mouth. "Really? You think that will work? Where were you all this time, huh?" My muscles tensed as I walked towards him with rage in my eyes. "Tell me! Where the fuck were you when I spent the last decade sitting in a fucking cage? Did you come see me? Did you call? No! You fucking didn't!”

The sound of a car rolling up the gravel caused us to pause. I turned my head and saw it was Charlie. *Why is she here? Shit. Not now! Not while he's around.*

The door opened and she hopped out with a smile. “Hey!” she yelled as she walked up, carrying a large plate wrapped in foil. “I brought you lunch.”

Even now, burning with unease, I was still touched by her gesture. “Thanks, you didn't have to do that.” As much as I wanted her there, I didn't want her around Brice.

“Don't worry,” she said. “I won't get you in trouble with your boss, I just wanted to bring you that. I figured you probably didn't have time this morning to grab something.” Noticing Brice, she turned towards him with a polite nod. “Hello.”

Brice wore an eerie grin. “Hello to you,

too."

Right there, I wanted to haul off and slug him across the face. I forced myself to smile, trying to joke with her. "Did you make it? Or should I really be thanking Sara?"

She hit my chest and laughed. "Alright, I'll let you get back to work. Talk to you later." She brought her lips to mine and kissed me gently.

I watched Brice from the corner of my eye as she walked back to her car. *Stop looking at her that way you dirty piece of shit. That's mine! I know what runs through your head.*

God, I want to beat the shit out of you.

You're not my brother anymore.

An evil smile spread across his face as he spoke. "So, that's your girl? She's pretty. *Real* pretty."

"Shut up. Leave now or you're going to regret it." My rage was turning red. If he kept up with these games I wasn't going to be able to hold back much longer.

"Look, Owen, I need your help. Now you can either choose to help me or I make you help me. I don't really want to hurt a pretty little face like that. But if it means my life or hers? Well, that's not a difficult choice." He kept his stare fixed on Charlie's car as it drove out of sight.

"What are you talking about?" A twinge of concern filled my voice.

"I told you, I have resources. I know more about you than you think. I also know where you were last night. *All* night. Think about it. I'll be in touch." He lit another cigarette as he climbed into a beat up, green truck out front. I stood and watched him fade into the distance.

He is going to use her against me. He can't do that! She is not on the table for him to use.

Shit! I don't even know what he could

be capable of anymore. Would he really put her in danger?

How? What is he thinking of doing? I won't help him! I can't!

I'd lose everything!

My mind raced with what had just occurred. He needed me to help him, but he thought threatening my woman was going to force my hand. I'd worked hard to stay clear of all that shit.

Then he had to show up and toss me back into his mess.

I wish he'd never found me. Fuck! Everything I have is being dangled over my head on a string.

Brice had given me a choice—but not really.

Was it possible to even choose between Charlie, my baby, and him?

I knew who I wanted to pick. I also knew Brice had meant what he'd said.

He'd hurt the things I loved.

What could he do to my new family?

Chapter Twelve

Owen

The spoon I held twirled around in my bowl of soup. I sat in a small diner up the street from the shop, hoping to clear my head.

I won't let him endanger Charlie. Brice is trying to use her as bait to get to me.

What could he be capable of?

"Hey, son, you realize you ordered that over an hour ago? It's probably cooled off by now." The small, elderly waitress cut into my thoughts. She rested her arm on the counter as she spoke. "You want me to get you a fresh bowl?" Her perfume reminded me of my grandmother. I didn't have many memories of her, I was young when she passed, but the smell of her perfume had stayed with me.

"Nah, I guess I'm not that hungry anyway." I pushed the worn, white dish away from me. "I'll just have another cup of a coffee."

I glanced over my shoulder to look out the window and mustered a half smile as I held up the empty mug.

He could be anywhere. Any time. I keep thinking he's out there, just waiting and watching.

As she refilled my cup her eyes met mine with a sense of concern. “Well if it's any consolation, I've been around and seen a lot of things. Whatever is bothering you, it'll find its place. Trust me on that,” she said, pulling the rag from her apron to wipe down the counter.

I shook my head. “I hope you're right.” I brought the freshly filled mug to my mouth and took a gulp.

She has no idea. How will this ever work out? I've been given an option from the devil; help him or he hurts my girl. What choice do I have?

Maybe we could run away? Pack our things and take off. We could move far from this place, start a new life on the other side of the country.

But would he find me? He found me this time, what's to say he couldn't do that again? If he's desperate enough and his life is on the line, what would stop him? I'm on parole still anyway, I can't just run away, that would get me locked up again.

In the back of my mind, something else kept prodding me. Brice had betrayed me, yes, and he'd abandoned me without ever explaining why.

But my soul had been imprinted by him. Blood ran deep, that was a fact.

Ultimately, Brice was still my brother.

That doesn't matter, I reminded myself. *You're about to start a new life, a new family.*

Charlie needs me.

If I decided to help him out of the mess he created, what would I have to do? Another burglary or something worse? Brice had a tendency to get involved with really bad people. If I joined him in this then my life could be on the line, too.

I can't do it, there's too much on my plate.

I had the opportunity to give a child the father I never had. If things went bad with Brice, then I'd end up back in prison. Who knew for how long this time, it could be the rest of my life.

Could I do that to this baby?

It seems the real choice he gave me is my life or his.

He is so fucking selfish, he always has been. When I was locked up, it was like I was invisible to him. Now all of a sudden he crawls out from the darkness and expects me to help.

What a joke.

He'd threatened to use Charlie against me, deep down I knew he was dangerous. I guess I'd just always hoped he'd forgotten about me, like I'd tried to forget about him. Obviously he hadn't. He'd just sat, waiting patiently for another opportunity to use me.

For how long? How long has he been following me, hidden from my sight?

I looked up at the clock, it was one in the afternoon. *Get it together. You have other things to worry about right now*. Charlie had an appointment with her doctor, it was the first ultrasound for the baby. If I wanted to be there on time I needed to leave. I'd told her I would go and I wasn't going to let her down.

I waved to the waitress as I chugged the last bit of coffee. “How much do I owe you?” I asked while pulling the wallet from my back pocket.

“Don't worry about it, honey.” She smiled and continued restocking the napkins.

“Thanks.” I threw a few dollars down anyway and left. The small bell above the door jingled as I exited to my car and a memory flashed into my mind.

I was fourteen, Brice and myself had been sent down to the corner store to pick up a few things for our dad. He had told us to be quick, a bottle of Jack and a pack of smokes was all he needed. Brice made the purchases and we headed back.

My dad had given us thirty dollars, all he had in his pocket at the time. “I expect all the change back,” he had said. I remembered his eyes were serious. They always were, I don't think he had a joking bone in his body.

As we walked back to the house, Brice pulled a pack of cigarettes out of the bag. They weren't my dad's brand. “Who are those for?” I had asked him.

“Me.” He slammed the pack against his palm a few times then opened them. He loaded one into his mouth and lit it.

I gave him a curious look. “Where did you get the money for those?” I knew he didn't have a job or any cash on him before hand.

“Dad's change.” He smirked and drew in a huge plume of smoke. “The way I see it, this is payment for making the run.” He let out a devilish laugh.

“You know he's going to be pissed.” I couldn't believe he had done that. Our father had the temper of a wild animal. But Brice didn't care. He had seemed to hit a point where he realized that it didn't matter what we did anymore.

The beatings came regardless.

We reached home and stood outside in the back so he could finish his smoke. I heard the sound of a bell come from behind us. When we turned around, there was my dad, holding the neighbor's dog.

He threw him down and came rushing in with a fury, swinging at Brice with his belt. “I told you to be quick! I told you I wanted my change! Could you do that? No! You ungrateful bastard!"

Brice dropped to the ground and cowered. I watched him beat my brother and when he turned towards me, Brice threw his hand out and grabbed his ankle. "No! He had nothing to do with it. Leave him alone!"

He protected me back then, kept me safe. And now he wants me to help protect him.

What kind of person would I be if I didn't?

I pulled into the parking lot of the doctor's office. *Clear your head, this is important. You want to be here one hundred percent. You can't be any place else.* I let out a deep breath and pushed my memories down into the cage I'd created for them.

As I looked up, I spotted Charlie. She had a huge smile on her face while she waved. She seemed even more beautiful today than ever; her skin was glowing as if fresh rain had sprinkled down on her. Her eyes twinkled with pure excitement.

I walked towards the front entrance and she ran at me. Her body hit me with such force I stumbled backwards. “Are you excited? I'm so excited! We're going to see the baby today!

My chest strained from my heart swelling. “Yeah, I'm excited. Nervous, too.”

“Yeah, me too.” Her hand wrapped tightly inside mine as the doors slid open.

I don't want anything to happen to her, or to our baby. I need to protect her, I'm here to keep her safe. That's my job now.

We took our seats in the waiting room and my heart pounded in my chest. It beat so profoundly I almost expected it to fly out from behind my ribs. Sweat beaded up on my palms and I could feel the nerves actually shooting between each other.

The room was filled with images of babies, diagrams of the female anatomy, and several other pictures that I had no idea what they depicted. "This is weird for me," I whispered into Charlie's ear.

"Relax, a lot of guys do this." Her smile was warm as she rested her hand on mine. The smoothness of her skin comforted me.

This woman is special. Everything about her draws me in, I've never felt this way before.

What the hell is happening to me?

If I had been asked a few years ago where I'd be right now, my answer would not have been sitting at the doctor's for an ultrasound.

The moment she'd told me she was pregnant, I'd promised that baby I would do everything in my power to give them what I never had.

I never break my promises.

A nurse opened the door beside us. She had a clipboard in her hand. "Charlotte?"

"That's me." Charlie stood and waved for me to follow. "Come on."

The room we entered was small, a paper robe was laid out on the table. Instantly, Charlie stripped down and put the uncomfortable looking gown on.

"That's what they have you wear?" I shot her a confused look.

"Yeah, fashionable, right?" Her giggle echoed in the cement room. It reminded me of the infirmary at the prison; solid concrete walls, a cold feeling permeating everything.

I sat down on the round roller chair. "What the hell are these for?" My hand reached up and touched a metal cup positioned on the end of a bar.

She smiled with delight. "Those are for my feet." Quickly, I pulled my hand from it. "You really have no idea what you're in for, do you?" She began to chuckle so hard she ripped the paper garment. Her breast fell out and we both laughed hysterically.

For the moment, all my worries washed away. I hadn't expected to ever find someone who gave me the feelings she did.

God, she's beautiful. I can't... no, I won't let anything happen to her. My brother can use me, he can threaten me, but he can NOT use her. No matter what happens, I'll make sure she's alright.

A knock on the door silenced us. "Well, it sounds like there is a party in here." A short woman entered with a grin. "Hello, I'm Dr. Hanson." She held her hand out to greet us.

"Hi, I'm Charlie and this is Owen." I nodded with the introduction and moved to stand beside Charlie.

"Well, it's nice to meet you folks. So, Charlie, you're going to get an ultrasound today. Are you ready to see your baby?" Dr. Hanson spoke softly. I had to lean in to hear her talk. "I'm going to have you lie back so we can check how the pregnancy is going and make sure it all looks good."

Charlie nodded to the doctor and brought her eyes to mine. Her eyebrows lifted with excitement, she smiled so broad all her teeth were visible.

I didn't know what to expect. Health class in junior high was one I'd always skipped out on. I knew my way around the female body, but what awaited me here was a guessing game.

Dr. Hanson rolled over a machine that was attached to a monitor. She brought the lights down low and pulled the paper away from Charlie's stomach. I sat silent, anticipating and trying to imagine what I would see.

What is she doing? Am I even going to be able to tell what is on that screen? My palms were clammy, my breathing intensifying as she squeezed a jelly onto the end of the mechanism in her hand.

"Alright, let's take a look. You guys ready?" She pushed herself closer to Charlie as her eyes met ours. Without words, Charlie nodded her head yes. She reached her hand out and grabbed mine. I felt her tremble in my grasp; I tightened my hand around hers and kissed her forehead.

A loud whirring filled the room as the doctor placed the device on Charlie's skin. The black picture turned a mix with gray. I stared at the image, trying to make out what I was looking at.

Is that... an arm? Holy shit. Oh my god, I can see the face.

That's my child. My blood growing inside her.

With large, open eyes I turned between Charlie and the screen. "Is that our baby?" My tone rode a wave of uncertainty from what I was looking at.

"It sure is." The doctor said. "See that

area pulsing quickly? That's the heart beating." She moved around on Charlie's stomach. The sound of white noise was integrated with a thumping sound. "And there are the arms and legs. The head is facing up."

Charlie had tears streaming down her face. "That's our baby, Owen. Our baby."

I brought my face to hers and kissed the salt stained skin. *Yes, our baby. My baby.*

"Well, everything looks great. With these measurements you're about thirteen weeks." Dr. Hanson pushed a button on the keyboard and a stream of pictures spilled from the machine. "Here you go, the first images of your baby."

Everything seemed so surreal, holding the photos in my hand I stared blankly at them. My mind raced with thoughts.

This is mine, my child

I'll be damned if someone is going to threaten them.

***

After the appointment, we decided to go out and celebrate.

Charlie had a craving for Mexican food. The restaurant was a small hole in the wall, close to her apartment. The food was alright, I'm not a big fan of tacos, but she had to have it.

I pushed the food around my plate, debating what I was going to do about the situation with my brother. After I'd seen my child, my decision seemed even more complicated.

If I help him, then maybe he will just go away. I could do this one favor for him, the last favor I would ever do for him. I could tell him that, make sure he understands that after this he would be dead to me.

No more help, no more saving him or

digging him out. This would be it.

But I can't! I don't want to risk what could happen to me. Charlie needs me, the baby needs me. What good would it do if I ended up locked up again? Or worse, dead?

Is he worth it? He's not.

But to save her, I need to keep her away from him. Away from the plague that follows Brice.

"Owen!" The loud yell she threw in my direction knocked me out of my daze. "Are you alright? You've been staring at your plate forever."

I met her glare with an empty look. "Yeah, I'm fine. Sorry, just a lot to take in." My eyes darted around the room, looking for any sign of Brice. I had been paranoid since his drop in. Knowing he had been following me, watching me, it made me uneasy. I had no clue when he would show up next.

Concern filled her face. "Look, I know

this is scary. And to be honest, I'm terrified. But after seeing the baby today my heart feels a love I've never experienced."

Her statement brought new meaning to what we had just seen. She was right, a certain unexplained love automatically swelled inside of me now.

I looked up at her, about to speak, the words teetering on the tip of my tongue. Then my eyes fell to the window behind her. Instantly, my insides began to shake.

In the reflection of the glass beyond her was Brice's face.

He smiled his crooked grin and waved. A rage instantly set in.

How dare he follow me? My fists clenched so tightly the nails left impressions in my palms. Suddenly, with a single blink, Brice's face was gone.

Did I just imagine that?

He's making me crazy! I'm seeing him

and he's not even there!

Sweat broke out on my flesh, distress immediately streaming over me. "I'll be right back." Swiftly I stood and walked towards the bathroom. Her mouth hung open behind me, unsure of what just happened.

My hands fell heavily on the sink, I peered at my image in the mirror. *Fuck, fuck, what am I going to do? I can't tell her what's going on. She has enough to focus on right now.*

I grunted loudly and gripped the sink. *He's like a parasite I can't get rid of! His face haunts me and all I want is for him to go away. How did my life suddenly fall into his hands?* My chest felt tight, my muscles tensed with internal fury.

Focus, get a grip. He doesn't control you anymore! Don't let him get to you. I inhaled a deep breath through my nose and exhaled out my mouth. I opened the door to head back, and there stood Charlie in the hallway.

"What the hell, Owen? What's going on?" Her forehead scrunched up.

"It's nothing, really. Let's go sit back down." I placed my arm around her shoulder and guided her back.

She slid into her chair to face me. "Owen, you can talk to me you know. Please, what's wrong? Are you really nervous about the baby? It's alright if you are." Her hands reached across the table, her fingers intertwined into mine.

I didn't want to lie to her, but I couldn't tell her the position I was in. The stress wouldn't be good for her or the baby.

I'm here to shield her from any danger. That's what I need to do. She doesn't have to know this, not now.

"Don't worry, Charlie. Everything's fine." My lip lifted awkwardly to the side. I looked behind her to see if the Brice-mirage was still present . She followed my eyes and turned to look over her shoulder.

The window was empty.

“You're being weird, Owen. You know I'm here for you, talk to me. You can tell me anything, I won't judge you or what you're feeling. Just tell me what's going on.” Worry filled her voice.

“Charlie, everything's going to be fine. I'm taking care of it.” I forced a soothing tone. “Really, I promise.”

I hoped it wasn't a lie.

But it still felt like one.

Chapter Thirteen

Charlie

Two days had passed since I had last seen Owen.

I found that strange since we had been inseparable for the past few weeks. When I called, he didn't pick up. Wanting to act like everything was normal, I decided I wanted to surprise him with dinner.

The store was a mad house when I went to pick up the food, it took a lot longer to check out than usual. I'd been trying to call him again since I left to head home, but the phone rang endlessly, each attempt met by his voice mail.

Where is he? This isn't like him, we've been connected at the hip since I told him about the baby.

Calm down, he's probably just busy at work. He'll call you back when he gets a chance.

A part of me felt ridiculous for being so upset over him not picking up. I knew my hormones were going haywire from the pregnancy. I had thrown a tantrum and cried the other day when Sara offered me a sandwich and she'd added mustard to it.

Stop, relax. A deep, warm breath lifted my lungs as I inhaled to try and slow my racing heart. *Just get home, you don't need to freak out while driving.*

I forced myself to focus on my surroundings. I watched the trees sway side to side, small buds could be seen starting to sprout from the bare branches, patches of snow had given way to the ground beneath. Winter was coming to an end and the feel of spring started to encompass the air.

I rolled to a stop at the red light, my window was cracked when the breeze crept through and caused me to shudder. It sent an unsettled feeling through my bones. I picked up my phone and dialed him again.

Never, even at work, has he ignored a call from me. The repetitious ringing filled my ear. *Come on, pick up already*. My finger anxiously tapped the steering wheel as I nervously peered out the window.

A click came across the other end and I sat straight up in my seat, hoping his voice would follow.

"Please leave a message for..."

]My thumb slammed the red end button.

Somethings not right. My heart felt heavy from worry while a nauseous feeling trolled my stomach.

What if he got hurt under a car or truck? What if something fell on him and he can't get help?

Maybe I'm just being a paranoid pregnant woman.

This isn't like him, I have to make sure nothing happened.

The rubber of the tires squealed as I made a sharp u-turn to head towards his shop. My foot pressed down on the pedal. I watched the speedometer rise as the engine roared to life with each shift of the transmission.

Come on, let's go! I hit my hand against the steering wheel with frustration.

I repeatedly kept trying his phone with no result. My body felt hot, like it was on fire from the fear that radiated through.

Alright, I'm close. His work is just a little bit further.

The dull glow of the sign started to come into focus. As I pulled up the dirt road the building was completely set in blackness.

What? Where is he? Owen always works in the evening. My eyes scanned the parking lot for his vehicle. *It's not here. Why is it not here?*

I threw the car into park and raced up to the front. I yanked on the door, but it was locked. My face pressed firmly against the small window, the inside was a blur of shadows with no movement.

I banged on the window with my open palm. "Hello?" I yelled. My open hand turned to a fist as I hit the window harder. "Hello, Owen?"

No one is here. His car isn't here, Bill's either. Where is he?

My legs shook as I walked back to my car. Heavily, my body fell into the driver's seat, disbelief setting in as I stared at the empty building.

Did he lie to me?

My hands reached up and grabbed the base of my neck as my eyes fell onto the cell phone resting on the passenger seat. I picked it up and decided to dial him one last time.

Every muscle tensed with anxiety, my stomach climbed the ridges of my throat. I almost dropped the phone from my grip with how intensely my fingers trembled.

The ringing was magnified in my ears, as if it was being played through a megaphone.

Answer, just pick up the god damn phone already!

Panic rushed in like a tidal wave when he didn't answer. I threw the phone down onto the seat and it bounced off onto the floor.

My head started to unhinge from any rational thought.

Why wouldn't be here? What is he really doing?

I could go to his house, but I've only been there once. I don't even know if I remember how to get there.

Owen had been acting different recently. I constantly watched him scan every place we went to, his eyes perpetually shifting in all directions. A paranoia seemed to weigh on his shoulders.

Maybe the pregnancy had created a

friction inside him? I hadn't been able to figure it out, even offering to listen got me no answers. The therapist me inside wanted to attribute it to the pregnancy.

Maybe he fears losing it all, losing the baby even? Does he worry he will turn into the father he barely had? He needs to open up, let me in. I might be able to help if he would just talk to me.

I should head home, maybe he'll show up there.

I gripped the shifter and pulled it hard into drive, but I struggled to click it into gear. *Come on! Not now!* With one swift tug it jolted into place; I slammed down on the gas and tore out of the parking lot.

The clock read five-thirty as I drove back home. My mind twisted with different reasons he hadn't answered or called me back.

He could be scared and second guessing about the baby, maybe he has doubts about being tied down?

All I know is he better have a good excuse for working me up like this.

As the tires bared down on the pavement I tried to calm myself. I didn't want to create an issue that wasn't there. I had thought about calling the police, but what would I say? That my convict boyfriend who is on parole hadn't called me?

What if he'd gotten caught up in something bad? He'd be sent right back to prison.

You're being crazy, Charlie. He's not doing anything, he told you before that he never wanted to go back. I'm sure he's fine. Maybe he left his phone in his car.

No, he always had it on him. Especially with the baby now, in case I ever needed anything. That's what he said, those were his words.

Something is wrong, I just know it is.

As I pulled into my driveway I noticed the apartment was dark.

Huh, I thought Sara would be home by now. Wait... no, tonight she's staying at her boyfriend's house.

The two had reconciled, continuing their pattern. It bothered me, but it wasn't my place to tell her who to date. Especially now.

The front door wasn't illuminated under the light. I fidgeted with the key, my brain tickling with a new realization. *It's way too quiet in there. Where's Biscuit? I don't hear him, he always gets excited when he hears me jiggling the lock.*

I opened the door and stepped in, my hand coming up to flick the switch in the entryway for the hall lights, but nothing happened.

Weird, what's wrong with the lights? I lifted the switch up and down a couple more times, but the hall remained shrouded in darkness. My hand rested on the wall as I made my way into the condo. The silence floated creepily around me.

What's going on? Why are the lights out? There hasn't been a storm or anything.

Did Sara forget to pay the bill?

As I reached the kitchen a loud thud echoed from further inside. My body, startled from the noise; no one was supposed to be home.

"Biscuit?" I walked in the direction of the sound. Slowly I felt my way down the hall, a subtle glow from the street lights outside casting shadows. I was able to see the shapes and outlines of where I was walking.

A noise I couldn't make out came from Sara's room. It sounded muffled and strained, I stopped in my tracks to listen.

Maybe she brought her boyfriend here?
"Sara? You in there?" My breathing began to intensify, worry and fear had set in. I could

hear something move around, but had gotten no response. “Hello? Sara? Are you home?”

A brief flash of a horror movie crossed my mind. Every time I watched one, I would yell at the screen for the girl to not make herself known, to be quiet and stealthy. I always thought they were stupid for yelling into the empty darkness.

But here I had been doing just that, yelling at something or someone I couldn't see.

Another thud crept through the air; I froze, uncertain of what I was hearing. Goosebumps riddled my skin. *I don't like this. Where are the lights? Where is my dog?*

As I passed the bathroom, an arm forcefully grabbed me around my neck from behind. I felt the cold metal of a blade against my skin and a man's voice filled my ear. “Be quiet and I won't slit your throat. Scream and it's all over.”

There wasn't a word strong enough to

describe what fell over me in that moment. Every muscle seized, my breathing became short and rapid. Instinctively I reached up and grabbed his forearms. *Who is this? Why is he here? What does he want with me?*

He pulled me in tighter against his chest and started to walk backwards toward the kitchen. “Don't fight back, got it?” The blade pressed firmly against my throat as he lit up a small flashlight.

I strained to speak. “Who *are* you?”

“Shut up!” He spat, pulling the knife away. “Try to run and I'll fucking kill you.” I heard him rustle something out of his pocket. The sound of duct tape being torn rang through my ears.

Think, Charlie, think. What can I do? Thoughts popped like bubbles in champagne, rising in my mind. My training as a therapist took hold. *Talk to him, try to befriend him. Make him look at you like a person and not an object.*

You have to do this for the baby.

"Why are you doing this?" I wanted to start off asking short, quick questions. See if I could get him to give me some information; try and piece together what his motives were.

"You're going to help me get something I need." He tightened his grip around my neck.

"What do you need? Money? I can get you money." I tried to keep my voice monotone and relaxed. I didn't want him to hear the terror I felt inside.

He released a loud, scratchy laugh. "You don't have the money I need, sweetheart. But, you're my ticket to getting it." He yanked my arms behind me to bind them.

"You don't need to do that," I said quickly. "I'm not going to run." I twisted my head up to see his face. In the dimness of the flashlight only his profile was visible.

He wrapped my wrists tightly in the

tape. “You bet your ass you ain't running. Now shut up and walk.” He pressed my arms into the small of my back and pushed me forward.

I stumbled forward. “How am I your ticket? If I don't have what you need then how can I help you get it?” I pushed my heels into the floor to slow down the pace.

He thrust harder against my arms. “Walk, and shut your mouth.” A pain seared up to my shoulder and I cringed. I felt the blade press firmly against my neck again, the tip only mere millimeters from actually piercing my flesh.

“You don't need to do this,” I said. ”Really, I'm sure there's another way! There has to be!” My feet dragged against the wood, trying to keep us in the house. I didn't want to go anywhere with this unstable stranger.

“*You're* my other way. You're my bargaining chip.” He leaned forward and opened the door. The knife lowered from my neck to the side of my stomach.

I had thought about running right there, but with the knife against my side, fear for my baby's safety hit strong. *Not yet, don't run yet. If you try to he could stab you.*

He could kill you and the baby.

The unknown man stepped beside me and locked one arm into my elbow. From the corner of my eye I watched him glance around nervously before walking towards my car. His hair was pulled back in a ponytail, an unkempt beard fell down over his chin. Was I wrong, or did he look familiar?

As we approached the car I searched for anyone I could motion to for help. Every condo seemed lifeless. When he reached for the handle of the car door, I realized I didn't have my keys on me.

He can't drive without them. When he realizes that, he's going to have to go back in and I'll run. I'm not going to be held captive by some asshole for ransom.

And I'm definitely not going to risk my baby's life.

To my disbelief, he pulled my spare set from his back pocket. My shoulders dropped with despair at the sight.

He opened the back door and shoved me in, eyes still scanning our surroundings. I landed roughly, scooting towards the far window, away from him. *Be strong. Clear your head, Charlie.* "Where are we going? At least tell me that." I started to push my questions. I needed answers.

"Didn't I tell you to shut up?" He climbed inside, starting the engine. The sound was like a chainsaw in my bones; every minute that went by, the more my chance at escape vanished.

"You did, but I still have questions. I think if you're going to use me I should get *some* answers. You can give me that, at least."

My eyes stayed firm on his in the rear-view mirror, I wasn't going to back down.

"I don't have to tell you shit. You mean nothing to me, but where we're going, you'll hold some weight." A smile twisted up on one side of his face as he let out a wicked laugh.

Again, I felt like I'd seen him before, but I couldn't place it. *Is he someone from the prison? It's happened to other therapists before; a crazed, unstable inmate fixating on them.*

Is that what this is?

I recalled a story where the woman's poor cat had been murdered and left on her doorstep by her stalker. My eyes welled up with the thought that he might have hurt Biscuit. "What did you do with my dog?"

"That little fucker is trapped in your closet. For a small dog he packs a sharp bite. Little shit bit me good. He's lucky I only kicked him." He lifted the knife from the passenger seat, the cold metal glistening under the passing street lights.

Eyeballing the blade, I swallowed around my dry tongue. “Are you going to kill me?” It was a question that I figured wouldn't be answered honestly, but it was worth trying.

His smile broadened, but that was all.

I looked down at the floor and noticed a glow from under the passenger seat. *My phone.* I'd forgotten that I threw it there earlier.

My thoughts started to race. *I need to get it somehow!*

His eyes locked on me in the mirror. I looked up quickly so I didn't draw attention to what I'd just realized. He didn't know it was there, and I didn't want him to find out.

I had to keep him talking, make him think and focus on my questions, not what I was doing. A sense of excitement and hope streamed through my body. “Why me?”

“Holy shit! You just don't fucking stop,

do you? What part of shut up are you not understanding?" His fists clenched the wheel tighter, the car careening down a small one way street. I watched the phone slide out of view.

Shit! No!

I couldn't see it any longer, but maybe... maybe I could still reach it. It was the only chance I had, I just had to be patient.

Staring out the window, I watched the road signs pass. Knowing where we were headed would be helpful, but I didn't recognize this area. The terror in my body swelled with each turn of the wheel.

I had no idea what was in store for me.

Chapter Fourteen

Charlie

The street lights had disappeared some time ago.

I hadn't seen a house or building in a few miles. The deeper we went into the cover of the trees the more fearful I became. *Where is this guy taking me? He's driving into the middle of nowhere!*

My eyes repeatedly shifted between his face in the mirror and under the seat. My phone hadn't come back into view, I wasn't sure how far under it had slid. *I need to get it, I could call for help if I could just reach it.* I dragged the edge of my foot around quietly under the seat.

I could see him watching me, taking in my every move. I didn't want him to become suspicious as I jostled around. If he started to think I was up to something, he might stop the car and look around, maybe find the phone. That was a risk I didn't want to take.

Quick, Charlie. Think.

"My arms are cramping up," I said. My face scrunched with discomfort as I tried to adjust my position. "Can't you just loosen this? It's really tight."

"Oh, your arms hurt, huh?" His voice was filled with a high pitched, teasing tone. "Well, too fucking bad." He rolled his eyes and shook his head.

Briefly, it had crossed my mind that this man might have kids of his own. If he was desperate enough to kidnap me for his own gains, maybe it was to help his family? *Knowing about the baby could pull whatever soul he has left to the surface. I can plead with him to just let me go, he might take pity on me and send me on my way.*

But, he could also not give a shit. Nothing I say will matter if he thinks he has nothing left to lose. What can I do? I need to protect this child!

He started to fiddle around in the pocket of his jeans, he patted it roughly then moved to the next one. I watched him nervously, unsure of what he was looking for. Eventually, he made his way up to the breast pocket of his tattered army jacket and pulled a pack of cigarettes from it.

He tugged one out with his mouth, resting both arms on the wheel to light it. "Want one?" He lifted the pack over his shoulder and let out a laugh. "Oh, that's right, you're tied up at the moment." The bearded man blew the smoke in my direction as he continued to chuckle.

"I wouldn't take one, anyway. I don't want anything from you." I glared at him from the backseat, wishing my eyes could burn a hole through his skull. Hesitating, I grabbed for the one thing I thought I could use. *Let him have a conscience, please!* "I also don't want you blowing your toxic fumes at me. It's not good for the baby."

The dashboard glow lit his eyes. They widened with surprise as his hand came down hard and smacked his knee. "Son of a bitch! You're pregnant?" Maniacal laughter exploded from his mouth, dissolving my hope. "Well, ain't that some shit. My brother went and got you knocked up! This is going to be good, then, really good!"

His brother?

No way, it can't be true.

My brain began to spiral with confusion as the man's face cemented in my mind. The crooked grin that spread across his face, his beady lifeless eyes; I *had* seen him before, but it wasn't at the prison.

He was at the shop that day I brought Owen lunch. Why didn't Owen tell me who he was? I stood right beside this dirt bag and didn't have a clue.

I knew that Owen didn't like talking about his brother, he avoided that topic completely. But, to know he'd decided not to tell me that his brother was right there, standing beside him... I thought he trusted me.

The revelation hit me with such force my breathing stopped for an instant. A pain in my chest began to surge, panic rocketed through every piece of my body. The fear I had felt enhanced to horror, not only for myself and the baby, but for Owen, too.

Did he do something to his own brother?

I hadn't been able to get a hold of him all day. Was my suspicion possible?

"Did you hurt him?" I blurted out. "You piece of shit!" I battled with the tape constricting my wrists, intensely I rubbed them back and forth against each other as if I was trying to start a fire. The burning sensation was numbed by my emotions, I just needed to get free.

He peered at me through the mirror, a look of satisfaction draped over his face as he watched me struggle. “We're getting close.” He dropped his head down, shaking it side to side. “I can't believe Owen got you pregnant.”

I continued to work at my wrists while we turned up a dirt road. I didn't recognize where we were at all, there was nothing but trees that seemed to span for miles. The tires crackled on the gravel as the forest gave way to a large clearing.

A small, rundown farm house came into view under the brightness of the headlights. The windows had been boarded up, the planks now hung partially off from decay. The roof was collapsed on one side and a tree was growing out from the gaping hole. It was apparent the place had been abandoned ages ago.

"What is this place?" My eyes took in the desolate surroundings. I knew that out here no one would hear me scream for help, no one would be able to find me if they came looking.

Is he planning on killing me? He could bury me out here and no one would ever find me.

The rawness of my skin stung beneath the tape. I had tried relentlessly to free myself, but still remained bound, unable to use my arms.

He pulled the car around the back of the house and cut the engine. The absence of light hid us in the shadows. "Now, we wait," he said, peering into the darkness.

Wait for what? What is he planning?

"Where is Owen? Did you do something to him?" I asked, glaring at him as I started to feel the tape stretch and loosen around my wrists.

I could see the outline of his face as he

turned to look over his shoulder at me. His expression was concealed in the night. “Just sit tight, sweetheart.” He opened his door and stepped out.

I was able to make out his figure under the moon light as he walked towards the side of the house, the black abyss swallowed him as he passed through the incandescent light.

Alright, come on. I stared out the window, watching for him to come back as I brought my hands under my body to the front. My mouth sunk into the tape like a wild animal on its prey. *I'm not going to be a victim here.*

The adrenaline pulsed through my veins as I tried to free myself, sweat beading up on my forehead while my eyes scanned the area. *Come on! Come on!* I spit pieces of torn tape onto the floor. Each piece was a step closer to freedom.

In the distance, the sound of an engine broke the silence. It roared up the abandoned road, the headlights shined so brightly they illuminated the entire area. My eyes narrowed from their intense glow. I tried to make out the vehicle through the holes in the decrepit building.

As the car turned and came to a stop, I caught a glimpse of Owen's brother leaning against the side of the house. I heard the muffle of voices, unable to distinguish who he was talking to.

Who the hell could that be? This isn't good! I need to get out of here and run.

The voices began to increase in volume. It sounded like Brice was yelling at the unknown person who had just arrived. Against the glow of the new vehicle I could see his figure walking back towards me.

No! Not yet! Frantically I worked at my wrists. Unable to free them completely, I quickly leaned down and felt around for the phone under the seat. *Yes!* I gripped the hard plastic.

Brice's shadow fell over the window and I shoved the phone into my pocket. He yanked open my door and forcefully grabbcd my arm. “You little bitch! Where do you think you're going to go? Get out!” He spoke through clenched teeth. If his tone had a color, it would have shined red.

He ripped me from the vehicle. I tried to pull back, tried to free myself from his grasp. “No! Let me go!” I screamed into the darkness, twisting and contorting my body in an attempt to break loose. His grip tightened around my arm as he dragged me through the grass and dirt.

As we approached the front of the house a figure was shrouded in the dark against the car. I watched his arms and chest puff out as my eyes made their way up to his face. The headlights cast enough light for me to see who had come to meet us.

Owen?

It's Owen!

Shock rested behind his eyes, they opened wide when I was brought into view. “What the fuck, Brice! Let her go!” His deep tone sliced through the night air as he took a step forward.

Brice dug his fingers harder into my arm. “I warned you, Owen. I told you I needed your help. You want to tell me no, fine. Now you need to say yes. Here is my insurance, no more fucking around!” Brice threw me in front of him, pushing me onto my knees, his hand still firmly grasped around my arm.

Owen's eyes fixed on mine for a moment, then rose to his brother's. “I'm telling you right now, let her go. I'm not helping you. I won't help you! And you're not going to do one god damn thing to her. I'll fucking kill you! How dare you threaten me and my family, threaten the woman I love?”

He loves me. I can't believe he just said that.

An evil smile filled Brice's face as he brought the knife out of his pocket. The metallic sheen glistened against the moon. “You don't have a choice, Owen. You're going to help me or I'm going to hurt her. And your child, too.”

I looked up at Owen with terror in my eyes. He had the appearance of stone; a feeling of security blanketed my body. I could see he wasn't afraid of his brother.

His massive figure constricted from the rage that Brice evoked.

He wasn't about to let anything happen to me or our baby.

Owen took another step forward and Brice took one back. He hadn't anticipated Owen challenging him and not giving in. “Don't make me do this, Owen. Just help me and all of this will be over. You don't understand how dangerous these people are. They want their money!"

Owen's fists clenched tight by his sides. His empty stare looked the same as the first day he was brought into my office. "Let her go, or you're going to regret it. I'm not considering your options, I'm giving *you* one."

I need to do something. I'm not letting this guy use me as a bargaining chip. My mind began to flurry with ideas of how to break free. Brice had the knife, but he was only focused on Owen. He wasn't looking down on me, he didn't have me in his sight at all.

This is my chance.

My head turned towards Brice's arm. Without a second thought, I leaned in and bit down hard on his flesh. He yelled in pain and instinctively released his hold, quickly I scrambled out of his reach.

Owen charged forward like a bull running into the red cloak of a matador. Brice's feet lifted from the ground and the knife flew from his hand. Owen landed on top of him, knuckles high in the air. He let his fist fall with all of his weight into his brother's face.

One after the other, the punches rained down.

Brice threw an elbow into Owen's jaw. “Get the fuck off me!”

The face of the man who loved me, who was here to protect me, was frozen with rage. His eyes looked black under the moonlight, his lip curled up on one side as his hands fell down repeatedly. It brought me back to the fight I'd witnessed at the prison.

But Owen was different, now. This time, he wasn't trying to save face or help someone who was weaker. There was meaning to this battle, it was a vendetta.

His freedom had been challenged, his family had been threatened.

Owen wasn't going to stand for that.

Brice struggled to gain back his control. "Look, we can talk about this! Man to man, brother to brother," he said. His eyes scanned the ground around him as he turned his head, trying to dodge Owen. "I wasn't going to hurt her, it was just to scare you!" Desperation flooded Brice's eyes as his hand rummaged through the leaves.

What is he looking for? Something glinted, catching my attention as the debris around it was disturbed. *The knife! He's trying to reach the knife!*

My eyes met Brice's; blood trickled from his mouth as he attempted to grasp the ground and pull himself towards the blade.

No, no god damn way! Without hesitation, I quickly ran over and kicked the knife out of his reach. Owen paused for an instant as he realized what his brother had been trying to do.

Twisting around, he hunched over Brice,

every muscle flexing. “You god damn liar!” He wrenched his shoulder back, slamming red knuckles into his jaw. “Talk it out man to man? And then you'd stab me, is that it?”

Years of pent up madness fell from each fist. A shallow grunt followed every strike. This was a moment that had been building for some time. While I didn't know the total history between these men, the tragedy—the betrayal—was obvious.

It hit me that my phone was still in my pocket. I pulled it out and started to dial the police. I worried that, if no one stopped him, Owen would murder Brice right in front of me.

“Owen!” Brice shouted. “I'm your brother! Stop!”

Owen lifted himself up high, his fist pulled back as he let one last blow connect. He stood over the beaten and battered man, glaring down on him with genuine hate. “No. You're not my brother anymore, Brice. And I'm not your little puppet, either."

Sitting up, Brice wiped at the blood staining his teeth. "Just this one time. That's it! They're going to kill me, man!" His eyes were as wide as they could go.

"No, I'll never help you again." As Owen spoke he stood taller. Turning towards me, he began to take long strides my way.

Brice reached his arm out, attempting to grab his ankle. "Please! I'll come clean, I'll clear your name, I'll go to the cops and tell them what really happened that night. That I was the one who killed that guard, that I was the leader of that job and you had only tried to stop me. You tried to talk me out of it! I'll tell them everything! Please! You can't let them kill me, Owen!" His voice shook as he spoke.

What? The words took a second to set in. *Owen didn't really commit that murder?*

I couldn't believe what I'd just heard. To find out that Owen had spent a decade locked up for a crime he didn't commit stunned me. All that time he had taken the fall for his brother.

But, why?

My eyes froze on Owen as this revelation came out. The words sat in my mind, unable to fully process. *He isn't the murderer everyone thinks he is. He was a brother just trying to protect his kin.*

And now he's here, protecting me, protecting his baby.

Owen looked down at Brice, disgust curling his lips. “I don't give a shit what you do, from here on out it'll never involve me. You understand?”

Brice rolled around, grimacing as he said nothing. Leaves clung to him from all the blood and sweat. Once, he tried to stand, but just curled over in pain instead. Light moans escaped his mouth as he twisted with discomfort.

This was a beaten man.

The danger he'd represented was gone.

Owen closed the distance between us. In the distance, sirens blared as they approached. "You alright?" He held out his hand, like he was going to pull me in.

I rushed forward, beating him to it. Clinging to his middle, I let out a long rush of relieved air. "Yeah, now I'm okay."

"Good," he said into my temple. "I just... that's such a relief."

His strength circled me, his nose in my scalp. For a minute we just held each other, our hands linking between us. Finally, I spoke up. "Is it true? You didn't kill that man years ago?"

His chest rose as he inhaled a deep breath, fingers gently brushing the hair from my face. "I wanted to save my brother. Just like he had saved me so many times. I fucked up though, Charlie. He used me over and over again. Same as he was trying to do now." He turned his head away and looked over at Brice.

"Why didn't you ever say anything?" I asked. This was difficult for me to grasp. For a person to spend that much time behind bars for a crime they didn't do, it made no sense.

"It took me a long time to open my eyes to what had really happened and the role I played. Who would've believed me anyway?" His head dipped as he spoke. "It doesn't matter anymore. It's over."

I placed my hand under his chin and brought his gaze to mine. "Did you mean what you said? That you love me?"

Taking my wrist in his fingers, he smiled lightly. "Of course. I love you, Charlotte Laroche. And I love our baby." His palm cradled my stomach possessively.

When he said my full name, my heart skipped a beat. I fell against him, our bodies as close as could be. His embrace felt perfect and secure; muscles that had just been used to defend me, now held my body with such delicacy. *This is where I belong, right here with him.*

The words floated effortlessly off my tongue. “I love you, too.”

He hugged me tightly, my cheek resting against his chest. My arms firmly clenched around his sides, unwilling to loosen my grip even as the high pitch of the sirens echoed through the trees.

Owen looked up at the approaching vehicles, his skin an alternating glow of red and blue. He pulled my waist in closer as we stood in the darkness.

I peered up at the handsome figure who was more than just a man. In the beginning, Owen had been my challenge. Then, he'd been my temptation.

Eventually he'd proven himself my hero.

And now...

He was my love.

Epilogue
Charlie

A year had passed since that horrible ordeal in the woods.

I sat on the front porch of my home, the beautiful sunrise warming my face when it shined between the breaks in the tree branches. *I'll never get tired of how peaceful it is out here in the morning.*

Owen's hands fell over my shoulders and squeezed them. "She's still passed out in there." He leaned in and kissed my neck softly.

A smile spread across my face as I brought a hand up to his. "Good, hopefully she sleeps for a while. It was a rough night." I sipped my coffee as he sat next to me on the porch swing.

Our daughter, Oriana, was born six months ago. Her name meant 'dawn.' She was a gift for both.

The first time I'd heard her small cry, my world changed completely. It was as if my eyes had been replaced by a new set. Everything shined brighter and stronger.

A fresh beginning to our new life.

We had decided to move to my hometown in Louisiana. It felt good to be back, surrounded by my family and friends. Everyone there was really accepting of Owen; it helped that they didn't have an inkling of what he was known for.

I'd decided to not tell anyone about what had happened to him or me. He deserved a completely clean slate, a place that wouldn't have eyes watching his every move. He had spent so much of his life in the headlines and under suspicion, he needed to be rewarded for the person he really was, and not who everyone *thought* he was.

After the police arrived that night and took Brice into custody, our lives didn't fall into place right away. You'd think that once someone else admitted to the actual crime it would be easy to just have it all erased for the innocent party.

Unfortunately, things aren't that simple.

The court system doesn't like being wrong. I spent countless hours in meetings with lawyers and in court, trying to get Owen's name cleared.

After three months of hearings and statements, it was all finally put to rest when his brother took the stand and grew the balls to do something right for once. He ended up being the key to erasing Owen's record.

Brice is currently serving life in prison for killing that guard, never mind the aggravated kidnapping.

I was finally able to watch Owen let himself relax and enjoy the life he had been given. He no longer had to worry about his brother trying to drag him back into the criminal underbelly.

We both had realized that there was nothing left for us in New England. His family ties had been severed completely, and I still had no job.

Sara had gotten an offer to work in Washington state. She didn't want to leave me homeless, knowing I couldn't afford the apartment on my own, but I encouraged her to go for it.

Despite his innocence, the town still treated Owen like he was a killer. They shunned him completely. Neither of us could go anywhere without hushed whispers floating behind our backs while people stared and pointed.

I didn't want to raise our baby in a place where people would constantly be judging us. I wanted to leave, move far away and start over.

And I did.

We did.

The click of feet shuffled against the glass door. "Biscuit wants out," he said as he stood and pulled the handle. Biscuit jumped into view, bouncing onto my lap before curling up in a ball. He rested his head against my thigh as he looked off into the distance.

"You love it here, huh, Biscuit?" I ruffled the fur that covered his eyes.

It had taken us some time to get on our feet. I'd been lucky enough to be able to ask my grandfather for some help; he let us live in the small apartment above the garage on his farm.

Then, I'd found a small office in town and opened my own practice.

The prison system was no longer a place I wanted to affiliate with. After everything I learned about what Owen had been through as a kid, it really hit me in the core. He'd spent his younger years fending for himself, he'd become a product of his environment.

There were so many young children out there dealing with similar histories of drug and alcohol abuse, I felt it necessary to try and focus on them. It seemed more ideal to try and give them the tools and support they needed before they got sucked into the dark side that would eventually ruin their lives.

"Do you have a lot of work today?" I asked, lifting my feet up and placing them over his legs.

He ran his fingers through my hair and twirled it around between them. "Yeah, I've got a few big jobs that need to get done. But, I'll still be at Oriana's six month check up today."

After the move, Owen had opened up his own automotive shop. He's really gifted with being able to fix and repair cars. The garage below us had been empty and my grandfather let him use it to get his foot in the door. His shop had been highly rated and was constantly busy.

Even with the demands his job required, Owen's first priority was our daughter and his family. I found it amazing to see this man and his love for his child.

She's the light of our lives, that's why we had chosen that name for her. Every sunrise meant a new beginning, dawn was the glow that started the day. Without it, there would be nothing but darkness.

The day she was born, Owen looked into her eyes and said something I will never forget; *A man will do very little for himself in comparison to what he will do for his family.*

Owen's hand ran down over my cheek, pulling me from my thoughts. My eyes took in how sexy and handsome he was. I tingled with excitement as his hand continued down my body. “How long do you think she's out for?” I asked with a wink.

A smile spread across his face. “I'm sure it'll be long enough.” He chuckled slightly as he moved Biscuit off my lap, leaning in to press his lips against mine.

His hand wrapped around my hip and he lifted me to straddle him. His cock was hard instantly as I lowered my weight. Owen's hands lightly draped the skin of my arms and a rush of chills flowed over my flesh.

God, I love him. He's amazing.

My head fell back as he drew small kisses across my neck and over my shoulders. His fingertips gently slid the straps of my nightgown down, exposing my breasts as a cool breeze drifted across my nipples, making them hard.

I brought my hands up and gripped his neck, pulling him in to suck on my breasts. The warmth of his tongue and delicate nibble of his teeth made me moan loudly.

"You like that?" he whispered into my ear as his hips shifted beneath me.

"I love that." My hand reached into his

pants and gripped his cock. I stroked slowly over his shaft and to the head, brushing the plush ridge.

His eyes closed and a heavy breath escaped his mouth. “Fuck, Charlie...”

“Guess *you* like that,” I teased, scraping my nails lightly over his balls. They tensed under my touch, and when I pumped his shaft again, I felt the slippery hint of precum.

His readiness had my center burning hot. Whatever patience I had was melting, my desire building up like a cement wall. Pulling his cock from his pants, I licked my lips at the sight of it. The early sun made it pinker, the thick flesh rigid and curved.

I moved my panties to the side, with one hand I spread my lips open and ran his swollen tip up and down my wet pussy. The shaft pulsed against me.

As I leaned in closely to his face, a hushed voice spilled from my lips. “Want to go inside?"

He lifted his eyebrows, nostrils flaring. "You fucking know I do." He held me tighter, pushing me forward so that I ground against him. The tip of his cock bumped my clit, and I gasped.

I couldn't take it, not any longer.

Adjusting my hips, I rolled my pussy over him; I was so wet he slid easily inside. Owen's hands gripped my ass firmly, he guided me up and down on him. His muscles tensed, almost like he had no control of them.

Owen brought his hand up and grabbed my hair, pulling down firmly, our bodies moving together in one fluid motion. The swing creakcd and shook as it rocked back and forth while we made love on the porch.

Leaning back, he arched his spine and growled. Watching how his shirt stretched, I slid it up, exposing the ink on his torso. I was compelled to touch the art, tracing the muscles and ink. Owen was incredible looking, I knew I'd never get tired of staring at him.

Inside of me, his cock twitched. “I'm going to cum, I can't hold it,” he said. Sweat glistened on his brow; I bent in to kiss it away.

Owen curled my hair in his grip, forcing me to meet his eyes. I froze, gazing into the depth of his irises, sinking in without wanting to return. “I love you,” he whispered.

It felt like his eyes were peering into my soul. Every inch of my body tensed. “I love you, too.”

His fingers dragged down over my bare back, following the indent of my spine. Then he caught my waist, using it for momentum, my pussy hitting down hard on his lap with each thrust. He lifted the front of my nightgown so he could watch his thick shaft disappear into the warmth of my soft, pink lips.

It turned me on to know he couldn't contain himself. Sparks of heat bloomed in my core, my body crushing—squeezing—as it shook with delight. The pleasure was immense, my heart so frantic I was getting dizzy.

A long moan exhaled from behind my lips as my orgasm hit. The wetness flowed over my thighs, my flesh riddled with goosebumps.

He was close behind me, panting so that it was all I could hear. With his palms embracing my ass, Owen gave a final thrust. He thickened, pumping into me with burst upon burst of cum.

I fell onto his chest, our breathing heavy as we stared into each others eyes.

He was meant for me. We were supposed to find each other.

A small cry escaped the open window above our heads. Biscuit ran up the porch steps and jumped onto the glass door, his ears perked to listen as he looked inside.

"See? Perfect timing." Owen's laugh radiated from behind his grin.

I was smiling, but I was too wrapped up in his existence... in the moment... to laugh. I couldn't pull my eyes from his. He had turned my world into the one I'd always wished for.

I couldn't imagine myself without him, and I didn't want to.

Once, Owen had said I belonged to him.

Now, I truly knew what that meant.

He's mine... I'm his.

We're chained together.

Forever.

THE END

ABOUT THE AUTHORS

Leah Holt

Growing up in a small town with little to offer, Leah Holt's imagination was able to run wild. She loves to write romance with intense alpha guys, the ones we all desire but dare not admit to. Who doesn't love a bad boy riddled with muscles and tattoos?

Having limited opportunities in life, writing has become an outlet for her to let out all of the dirty, forbidden thoughts inside of her head.

If you want to chat with her, you can email leahholtauthor@gmail.com , or click the mailing list link below to receive information on her new releases!

Nora Flite

A USA Today Bestselling Author, Nora Flite loves to write dark romance (especially the dramatic, gritty kind!) Her favorite bad boys are the ones with tattoos, the intense alpha types that make you sweat and beg for more!

Inspired by the complicated events and wild experiences of her own life, she wants to share those stories with her audience. Born in the tiniest state, coming from what was essentially dirt, she's learned to embrace and appreciate every opportunity the world gives her.

She's also, possibly, addicted to coffee and sushi.

Not at the same time, of course.

Check out her website, noraflite.com, or email her at noraflite@gmail.com if you want to say hello! Hearing from fans is the best!

Made in the USA
Middletown, DE
19 April 2017